THE GOLDEN BOWL

A NOVEL BY FEIKE FEIKEMA

The Golden Bowl

GROSSET & DUNLAP

Publishers   *New York*

Published by arrangement with The Webb Publishing Company

". . . that longing, peculiar to man, which makes him reach out toward infinity; and he lifts up his eyes, and he strains his eyes, looking across the ocean, for certain fabled, happy islands; . . . and all his days he journeys through the world, spying about him, going on and ever on, expecting beyond every hill to find the holy city . . ."

—Arthur Machen
HIEROGLYPHICS

THE GOLDEN BOWL

I

TWISTING ITS WAY AMONG FAT BLUFFS, the Highway
reaches the Sioux River, crosses it, and enters eastern
South Dakota. It turns sharply west on prairie farmland
toward a cloud of treetops on the far horizon, which,
lengthening, become towering cottonwoods. The steeples
and smokestacks of a city come into view.

The Highway hesitates beside red-and-yellow gas sta-
tions and oily hot dog stands. It enters the city, slips between gaudy super-markets housed behind the false fronts
of old stores, runs beneath elms that spread leafy wings
over high frame dwellings, and then sprints westward on
a level plain.

During the early thirties the land around the city and
some way west was green in May, though here and there
the grass and corn were flecked with dying yellow blades.
For a few miles, too, the buildings sparkled with paint
and shining window panes. The cylinders of water-towers
loomed above the little towns, glossy as stovepipe hats.

But farther on, the land had lost its healthy green.
Some of the leaves were pale and some of the stalks were
yellow and dead. And many were brown. The water-towers and windmills, and the barns and silos and houses
and coops, and privies behind the windbreaks, became
more drab, more deserted, the paint more chipped and
gray.

Gray dust filmed everything, even the moving things.
When the wind came, the old structures shrugged a little
and the gray silt slid off in shivers. And sometimes, when
a rain would come, the old buildings stood forlorn
amidst the rustling of strange greens.

The Highway lopes through this land, curving some-times, and cutting sharply, but always running west through South Dakota.

During the drouth years it passed dying farms and bonesharp people. It spanned the dry beds of vanished rivers marked only by rows of leafless trees. It crossed the lazy James, asleep in the roomy bed once occupied by the old Missouri. It circled empty lakebeds that lay cracked and ugly, and only a little damp, like the crust-ing sores of eczema.

It passed dry wallows where, centuries ago when the land was covered with knife-edged prairie grass, buffalo romped and gored.

Empty wells pitted the land. Rotting bodies of dead animals lay facing empty water tanks. Skeletons of farms lay quietly in dusty slumber. Machines, the levers once warm with the cupped hands of men, stood idle, rusting, blackening.

Fissures in the land as deep and wide as glacier cre-vasses opened the soil to the wind. Cracks wide enough to swallow cows zigzagged across the earth like strokes of black lightning. The earth, like a colossal apple hurled upon the floor of the universe, had burst open, its frag-ments scattering to the winds.

The Highway winds among these things and runs west.

Suddenly it comes to where the Missouri River has gouged a deep diagonal wrinkle across the belly of the state. It dips sharply into a small valley, pushes through a little town, and hastens to the edge of the Missouri River banks. A bridge arches over the muddy water and on the other side the road climbs again and moves stead-ily westward.

It rolls through a land heaving with an ocean's undu-lation. It skirts the edge of Big Foot Hill, where a spur

4

drops abruptly into the yawning, rasp-rough mouth of the Bad Lands to snake its way among the myriads of red-yellow teeth.

At last, near the western border of South Dakota, the Highway moves quietly beneath the blue pines of the Black Hills.

Somewhere between the Missouri and the Bad Lands, the Highway suddenly turns south, then west again.

Here, long ago, it was only a path which curved to a creek. On this path, mule-eared jackrabbits sometimes leaped out of the tall prairie growths to sit in the open sun, ears keen to the wash of the wind in the grass. Field mice scampered over the soft earth. Clear, quick winds ruffled the sharp grasses, and crickets and grasshoppers hurtled themselves into the density near the ground.

Partridge and prairie chicken ran across the path in swift formation. Antelope and cottontails bobbed across it. Prairie dogs yelped on it. Turkey buzzards and prairie hawks soared and banked above it, a-hunt for fallen life. And in the dusk when the great horned owl sounded its doleful cry the path became treacherous with coyote, fox, and wolf.

And other creatures shared the path with the wild life. The pattering of feet and the beating of horses' hooves on the drum of the earth frightened the animals. First it had been the friendly, talented Arikaras, then the imperial Dakota Sioux, silent and hawk-nosed, who swiveled along the path, looking ahead, watching the horizons, ears sharp for sounds of stealth. Squaws, laden with food and shelter and young, followed. And behind, running, came bright-eyed children, and tired dogs with red-wet, slippery tongues.

Eventually the white man came and looked at the land with long eyes. Then the iron-shod hooves of white men's horses and roughly-cast wagon wheels cut into the bed of the trail and the grass at the sides. The settlers came.

One among them, a red-haired man named Iver Thor, stopped at the jog in the path and surveyed the land. Here, he told his blond wife, Thelma, they would unload their wagon and stake their claim.

He built a sod shanty and cut lumber for his barn from the cottonwoods along the creek. Ignorant of the land, the sky, the sun, and the capricious and subtle interweaving of their forces, he broke the prairie sod.

Time rolled on and clouds of days trailed their rain of events over the green fields and the pasture and hay land. A son was born to the Thors, whom they named Tollef, and a daughter, Kirsten.

A two-room house built of willow wood replaced the sod shanty. At night, in the clean square rooms, Tollef and Kirsten whispered and wondered and dreamed. The land was green with wheat, corn, pasture, and hay. Rains came like womanhood, full in the spring and early summer, sparse in the autumn. Corn and wheat kernels were heavy with milk. Iver, Pa Thor, watched the stars and counted the days of his work. Thelma, Ma Thor, baked and patched, and kept her children from harm.

But there came a spring, and then a summer, of long days when no clouds came, and no rain, to lessen the heat of the sun.

And the wind came. Clear at first, it rolled and lifted, blustered hard and blustered soft. The wind raked the land. The sun parched it. The wheat, corn, pasture, and hay land became yellow, then brown, then black. The land hardened, fissured, broke into lumps, into powder. The once-clear wind became a bronze wind that shadowed the land as it beat upon it.

Pa Thor cut a new hole in his belt, and Ma Thor

fashioned larger patches for the worn clothing and thinned the gruel. Tollef and Kirsten, now as tall as tasseling corn, stirred restlessly in their sleep at night.

The next spring Pa Thor loosened his belt, oiled the harnesses, sharpened the discs and harrows, and cleared his voice at breakfast to plan the work of the day. Hoping-time had come again.

But May came again with no clouds. And June.

And the dust came again. Dust that filled the sky, the fields, and the rivers. Dust that choked the lungs of the men and the cattle.

The Thors fought the grim force silently day by day, and often at night.

The rich earth to which the white man had come began slowly to vanish in little running feet of dust that sprinted over the ground, in dried silt that raced over the fields and beat on the buildings and on the faces and bodies of men.

When Pa Thor could not meet the taxes, the Government took back all the land but the home farm.

And then the assets of the bank dried, too. There was no more credit.

Pa Thor and Tollef returned from town with the news, grim and silent. They left their few purchases on the front steps for the women to take into the house. Then they stalled the horses, hung up the harnesses, and sat and pondered together. They fumbled absent-mindedly with the hay forks, rubbing the work-polished handles with calloused hands. They flipped the forks aimlessly, remembering the days when, beneath a pleasant sun and a clear sky, they had burdened the tines with bundles of gold-stalked grain.

Then they bestirred themselves. Ma Thor and Kirsten would have to know sooner or later. Their chins jutted out and their neck muscles tightened. They opened the barn door and solemnly marched toward the house.

Ma Thor, watching from a window, saw them stalking toward the houseyard gate and quickly waved Kirsten about. She warmed the coffee on the stove.

Silently, purposefully, Pa Thor and Tollef stepped through the door. They drew chairs to the table, hooked their caps on their gaunt knees, and wordlessly stirred the black coffee.

Ma Thor looked up from her cup and searched the men's faces, then dropped her glances to their shoulders.

Pa Thor carefully lighted his corncob pipe. Then he looked up. "Nothin'," he said tonelessly. "Nothin' no more."

Ma Thor studied his face, then Tollef's. "No?"

"No."

"Well, what then?"

Pa Thor shrugged. "I dunno. Relief from the Guv'-ment maybe." Then, "An' why not? They took some of our land for taxes. Their turn to give now."

Ma Thor bristled, then said, "Have the Thor men become calves that they'll take tit from a cow?"

"Well, it's that or . . ."

"There'll be none for me and Kirsten!"

Pa Thor paled. "Hold your tongue!" he shouted.

Ma Thor and Kirsten washed the dishes and pans in silence. They waited for the men to cough and to talk some more. They washed slowly, drying the plates and the cups again and again.

Soon Pa Thor coughed.

The women waited.

Pa Thor scratched a match. "Guess you're right, Ma," he said at last. "The banker said 'No.' The grocer said 'No.' Well, we can say 'No,' too. No! We won't go with them that's on relief. An' we won't follow them that's gone to Californier. We'll stay put!"

Ma Thor said nothing. She wrung her towel. "Anyway, we'll try her once more."

The stone-toothed wind hid the face of the sun and fretted and taunted the earth. Dust beat on the grain and killed it. Dust beat on the animals and choked them. Dust battered the barns and the houses. It beat on the brows and the backs of the people, on the Thors and all their neighbors.

When the Thors had only tumbleweeds growing on their land, Pa Thor, always an inquisitive man, culled green prickles from the Russian thistles and brought them to Ma Thor, who boiled them for gruel.

"Not bad, Tollef," Pa Thor said. "Not bad. Better than nothin' by far. The stuff tastes good."

But when Pa Thor and Tollef fed the prickles to the animals, the cattle and horses became gaunt.

The wind drove and the sun burned, drying and cracking and breaking the land.

Pa Thor and Tollef searched ceaselessly for water. They tried forks of willow twigs held upside down in the hands, the deep intentness of prayers at the table, and shrewd guessing. But there was no water. Thirsty animals bellowed and whined. Some gasped and died, to have their bones cleaned by the coyote and the wolf. Those that lived tramped the empty beds of rivers, nuzzled the empty water tanks, and sometimes, like dogs, dug at the mucky wells.

When the long arm of the Government reached for the hungered animals, Pa Thor and Tollef, with thinned and furrowed eyes and stubbed and beaten brains watched the old herd go.

The great wind roared with greater fury. Dust drifts

wavered around and over the buildings, the machines, the homes, the chalky bones of cattle, and the path to the privy in the leafless orchard.

The Black Blizzard of November, 1933, had come.

On the first night of the storm, Tollef lost his way and wandered over the desert's howling floor. In the doubly black night, solicitous of the animals, he had tried to walk the short way from the house to the barn. Two days later, when the wind let up, they found his body in a drouth-crevasse near the willows by the creek, smothered in a drift of flour-fine dust. Like a mountaineer on a glacier in a blizzard, he had not seen the yawning chasm ahead.

Dust drove through the cluster of bareheaded people that gathered in the churchyard. Dust filmed his coffin. Dust and the minister's word fell beside him in the grave.

II

In 1934, a faint pulse beat in the dry breasts of April's clouds and gave the Thor farm a week of indifferent rain. In the new water of spring, the wrinkled prune-skin of the earth swelled a little, and became smooth again. And the fissures and cracks began to close.

And vein roots swelled. New sprouts came. And the land, suddenly and incongruously, resembled an old man's face covered with a young man's fuzz.

Sucker stems at the roots of the trees and the bushes grew quickly. Bright leaves flowered on an occasional lower branch, but the upper limbs, out of the reach of the weakly rising sap, remained snake smooth.

Pasque flowers purpled in the draw. Gumbo lilies bloomed out of the dark hardpan clay. Yellow petals of elephant-eared cactuses dotted the lowlands.

The bed of the creek west of the barn became black with new damp, and pale green with many quick-nursling weeds. Slowly a stream grew, tugging at the new roots and at the black soil, uncovering a layer of sand.

But May came with no rain. And though the lands were still green with weeds and sprouting grain and corn, and the pastures were still blue, the air became dry. The wind rose. Each day it became stronger. Dry patches widened on the hills. Clouds of gray dust began to chase shadows over the land. The water in the creek slowed to a trickle. The leaves of the willows fell.

The Thor farm sagged limply on the turn of the Highway. The two-room shack was paintless. A gate facing the road creaked and the path it once straddled before the shack lay buried beneath last year's dust-drift.

Beyond the house and to the west, the tough old barn, also paintless, leaned crazily on one knee beside a once-rich manure pile now a shriveled, scaly crust. A burlap sack snapped in a window.

Leafless trees lining the banks of the creek clawed the drifting murk like some grubworm thrown on its back. Beyond, an old wooden windmill frame, like the skeleton of a dinosaur, lay bleaching in the sun. Distantly, telegraph and telephone poles stalked across the country.

North of the shack, immaculate rows of semi-bare trees ran in a straight line. Far beyond, like the hull of a voyaging ship on an ocean, the black tank of a water-tower sailed close to the horizon.

East of the housegate, where a washout, or gully, turned with the Highway, the roots of a tree-stump hung octopus-like from the gully's upper fringe. The skull of a cow, a broken wagon-box, an old bedspring, and other metal scrap littered the floor of the gully. From the gully on, the land unrolled, mile on mile, to a vague horizon.

To the south, green and gray-brown prairies stretched endlessly away, sometimes lifting like swelling seas.

Dusk came gently. The wind rested in the fields. A haze of dust in the air deepened the purples of sunfall into a dark red.

A young man walked west on the graveled Highway through the gritty dusk. He paused sometimes to shift two bundles on his shoulders. Every few steps he thrust out his lean head, looking to the side of the road and at the fields.

The man stopped at the turn, studied the shack intently and then examined the washed-out gully. Then he slid with a clatter down the side of the washout, holding one bundle carefully in his hands. He laid it gently on a soft dust-drift.

Unrolling the other bundle, which he handled roughly, he pulled out a can of beans. Two tumbleweeds were
caught in the roots of the tree-stump above him. He
reached up, pulled them loose, crushed them in a neat
pile on the floor of the gully. Cupped fingers over a
match kept out the downdraft of wind. Suddenly, the
tumbleweeds spat lustily, lighting up his face and his
body and the sides of the gully.

The old, broken wagon-box offered dry boards. Quickly, he loosened a piece and, half-squatting, broke it over
his knee. He built a pyramid of kindling over the fire.

A long wagon-rod lay beneath the skull and he drew
the rod up and from it fashioned a crosspiece above the
uprush of heat. He worked carefully, balancing the beans
on the crosspiece.

His worn blucher shoes creaked with each move of
his body. Long, thin muscles and heavy bones gave him
an incisive appearance. His face was smooth and a little
hollow, and little wrinkles ran lightly off the edge of his
eyes and beneath his temples. Dry, stiff hair spurted from
under the side of a cap cocked easily over one ear. Much
wear had hiked the visor of his cap. His eyes were sharp,
almost hidden behind a squint. His lips were thin, almost cruel, though his gestures were kind. Dust empha-
sized the faded blue of his overalls and of his denim
shirt.

He was about to settle before his fire when the gate
creaked above him. He turned to listen closely. Presently, after relating the noise to the gate, he relaxed. He
searched the dump until he spotted a rusted skillet. He
picked it up and shook out the dust. He held it against
the flames to hunt for holes. There were none. He
reached for the beans. They were hot, now, and he
cursed his scorched fingers. He opened a jackknife and
cut cleanly through the hot metal. The dull blade

squealed and raised little shivers along his spine. He shook the beans carefully into the skillet and set them over the fire.

The heat of the fire set up a sizzle in the beans. The seeds in the tumbleweeds popped. Slowly the wood caught fire along the edges. Soon the tumbleweed flame died. And then the wood flames hesitated. A gust of wind brushed the fire. Smoke swirled thickly for a moment and then cleared above a good flame.

The man sat hunched before the warmth. The gully sparkled with light; and dust particles, falling through a dying wind above, sometimes glittered.

Presently the man stirred, unrolled the other bundle, opening, first, a burlap sack, then an oilcloth roll, and then a guitar case. He lifted the guitar tenderly. His mouth leveled and softened. His eyes nearly closed.

The man fingered the strings softly, testing and tuning, tightening and releasing the pegs. He looked up then, searching for a tune with his fluid fingers. He hummed, and then broke into a whispered song, bending over the pound of the full chords, forming new words as he played along—

> *I'm a tumbling, tumbling, tumbling weed.*
> *'Ling weed . . .*
>
> *Just a rambling, rambling gant hay seed.*
> *Hay seed . . .*
>
> *I'm a grumbling, grubbing bindlestiff.*
> *Ol' stiff . . .*
>
> *Just a wand'ring, wond'ring thistle weed.*
> *'Ling weed . . .*

The man's face mellowed. His eyes became luminous, his thin lips molded the words with care. His caressive fingers wove liquid patterns on the strings. The man was deep in the story of his wanderings—

14

Came on alone here.
Had a can of seeds.
Built a little fire
Out of tumbleweeds.
Tumble . . .

Been rollin' all day,
Been tumblin' all week.
Hit a hole in clay
An' tumbled down weak.
Tumble . . .

When the wind blows west,
I tumble on, tumble.
When the wind blows east,
I tumble on, tumble.
Tumble . . .

The beans sizzled loudly in the fire. The gate creaked. As he rocked rhythmically, his shoes squeaked, curiously in harmony with the low beating chords. Curt little winds skirted the edge of the gully and spilled fine dust over his face. He hunched over further.

Abruptly, above him, footsteps crunched in the sandy soil. The man's fingers fell on the strings. The footsteps came closer and halted.

The man lowered his guitar disgustedly, and then called, "Well, come on." He carefully wiped the dust off the guitar and rolled it back into the oilcloth.

When no one moved above him, he looked up, asking, "Well?"

An old man stood looking wistfully down at him. The old man wore a black hat. Brown and gray tufts of hair protruded from beneath it.

The guitar man looked up at the old man on the brow of the gully a moment and then said, "Well, come an' get it. C'mon." He turned to the fire again, stirring the embers. "Every time I wanna be alone, some bastard has to come along and grub with me. Damn funny thing."

"Hello, son," the old man said, looking at him curiously.

The man in the gully stood up, shading his eyes to look at the other. "Howdy."

The old man said, "Saw your fire and thought I'd come out and see what was doin'."

"Oh. You live there?"

"Why sure, son."

"Christ, I thought the place was deserted."

"Why, that place ain't deserted, son. Three right lively people livin' in it." The old man's eyes studied the stranger searchingly. Then he said, "You look like you might be a farmer's son."

The man laughed a little. The old man's staring made him feel awkward. "Well, you're partways right. I was, once."

"A farmer's son! What's your name? Mine's Thor."

"Grant. Maury Grant."

"Pilgrim hereabouts?"

"Yeh."

"Lookin' for work?"

"No." Maury squinted his eyes to get a clearer look at the old man.

"You ain't?" the old man asked with some surprise.

"No." Then, "What makes you think so?"

"Well," the old man looked down and scuffed his feet in the gray-black dust, "I dunno. I'm lookin' fer a boy to work fer me. I need help. My son Tollef died last year."

Maury studied the old fellow for a few moments, then suddenly said, "Well, 's a matter of fact, I am lookin' fer work. What've you got?"

The old man's eyes lighted with an almost holy light.

He said, "Why! I got a farm, son."

"A farm?"

"Sure."

Maury glanced dubiously at the buildings. "Where?"

"There," and the old man pointed.

"Christ!" Maury ejaculated. "No, I'm afraid you ain't got work fer me." He settled on his heels again.

"Why not?"

"Not in the dust bowl."

"Why, this ain't a dust bowl. It's good farmin' land."

Maury snorted. "Farmin' my foot! It's hell, that's what it is. No. No dustbowl farmin' fer me . . . ever again."

"Oh."

Maury worked around his fire a little. The old man annoyed him.

"You won't work fer me, then?"

"No! Hell no!"

"Even fer a while?"

Maury stood up again. "Lissen," he said, "I don't know what's wrong with you, but I know fer sure that I ain't workin' in a desert. I got my guts and lungs full of it once down in Oklahoma, and I've had enough. I'm gettin' outa here quicker'n a jackrabbit with its tail on fire. Goin' where things stay green."

The old man sighed and looked forlornly at Maury. "But I gotta have help," he said, "an' you bein' a farmer's son an' all, I thought . . ."

"Well, fer Christ's sake!" Maury whispered to himself, "It's got him. He's loco." He shook his head. "The dust'u got him just like it got Pa." Then, looking up, he said firmly. "No, Mister, you're lookin' at the wrong guy. Sorry."

The old man stood motionless on the brink of the gully for a long time. Then he said, "Mind if I set with y'u fer a spell?"

Maury laughed. "Hell no," he said, "I'm the guy that should be askin' you. Mind? I'll vamoose pretty soon—an' stomp out the fire."

Pa Thor slid down the bank. "Go ahead. I just come out to see if you didn't wanna work." He watched Maury closely for a response, then went on. "As I always say to my daughter, Kirsten, y'u kin never tell when a bum'll come along an' take some work."

Maury grunted. "Huh! Or some chickens."

The old man shook his head. "Oh, no," he said, "Nobody 'd steal my chickens. Might take one to eat, but that wouldn't be stealin'."

Maury studied him covertly. The old man pushed back his faded hat and wiped his brow. His face quivered with many wrinkles. His movements were slow. Crow's-feet at the corner of his eyes gave him a quizzical expression, and his eyes sometimes became dreamy.

Pa Thor groaned and, holding his back, settled on his heels. He stared at the fire. Finally he said, "How about a cup of coffee with them beans?"

"It'd be all right." Maury leaned forward from his crouch to taste the beans, gingerly picking up a few with his fingers.

Pa Thor said, "If you c'd see yer way to doin' a little work, I'd get the wimmen to fix you a meal."

Maury shook his head. "No. Never mind. Meal sounds all right, but not the work."

"You wouldn't like a warm meal?"

"Not that bad."

"The work won't be hard, son."

Maury shook his head.

Suddenly Pa Thor said, "Tell you what. You kin stay the night if you want."

Maury looked directly at him, squinting his eyes. "You mean you're offerin' me a bed?"

"Yes."

"A real bed?"

"Well, it's a cot. Sure, a bed. Don't you like cots?"

"Sure."

"Well, then what's wrong with it?"

"Nothin'. Just seems kinda funny fer a guy to offer a stranger a bed."

Pa Thor looked down, rocking on his heels and sifting dust through his fingers. "Well, it's like I been tellin' you. I'd like to have a man around here. Gets lonesome. 'Specially when you need help."

"No other menfolks around?"

Pa Thor smiled, and said, "Well, I got a friend over at Sweet Grass," he motioned over his shoulder northward, "an old feller, name a Ol' Gust. A well-driller. But Ma Thor won't let me see him very often. Oh, she don't beat me up or anything, but she don't like him." Pa Thor paused and watched the dust sifting through his fingers. He laughed. "Great guy. Never married, but a heller with wimmen. Likes his likker, too. I sneak out to see him once in a while."

Maury rolled a cigarette and handed the tobacco and papers to Pa Thor.

Pa Thor took the makings and fingered them absentmindedly.

Maury lighted his cigarette deftly with a glowing ember and replaced it in the fire. His sandy hair fell over his forehead and he circled his cap a few times with quick jerks to imprison the locks again. He looked at Pa Thor speculatively. "An' no one else around?"

Pa Thor shook his head. "Nobody. They've all pulled out fer Californier, or somewhere. There ain't nobody livin' to within ten miles, 'ceptin' the skinny Graysons. And they're too dead to know they ain't dead yit. Nope, the dust and the hoppers has driven nearly everybody out. We've held out because we got a crick west a here. Sometimes it has runnin' water an' the land gets a little moisture."

Maury picked up a handful of dust and studied it. "This dirt don't look like it'd make good farmin' land."

"Oh, but it does!" the old man exclaimed. "Damned good land."

"Looks like hardpan clay to me."

"Oh, no, that's not hardpan clay. It's gray-black sand loam, mostly. You an' I are sittin' on a table-land of it. Grows pretty good. Very good. Gets greasy when it rains. An' when it gets too dry it weathers to a yeller-gray color like this."

"Why, that's gumbo."

"Sure."

Maury squinted at the dust. "I heard somewhere, think it was the Guv'ment, that all this land should go back to grazin'. Like it was when the Indians and buffaloes had it."

"Poppycock!" The old man snorted. "That's them Guv'ment fellers fer you. Always runnin' at the mouth, and most times wrong. I've farmed all my life, an' I know farmin'." He paused. "Yeah. First it was the ranchers that tried to get us out. Then the hoppers. An' now it's the dust and the Guv'ment. But we're hangin' on. An' we'll stay on. This is a wonderful good country fer farmin' an' it'll be all right next year."

Maury puffed slowly, sifting dust with his free hand. He looked at Pa Thor. "Comin' along here tonight, I thought I saw a little green on the fields. Had some rain?"

Pa Thor nodded eagerly. "Yeh. We did. Sure did. Got some corn an' grain started. Pasture's a little blue so's the cows kin eat a little." Suddenly he sat up and listened.

20

"Hear a car?" Maury asked, rising a little. A ride would end this awkward conversation.

Pa Thor shook his head. "Guess not. Must be one a my two cows." He paused. "I got two left. Guv'ment took the rest. Got two horses an' a few chickens. An' a sow ready to pig. She's late. A little grain, too. Got two wells, both about dry. Had a windmill once, but the wind took that last fall an' rived it smack through and drug it across the country. Yep, we're down to where the hair's short." He rolled his cigarette mechanically. "But we'll make it." Then, "If I can only get a man to help me."

Maury settled again and stirred his beans with his jackknife. "You said somethin' about some wimmen?"

Pa Thor licked the roll of paper and twisted the end. He leaned forward and lighted the cigarette with a little flame along the edge of the fire. "Ma Thor and my gal, Kirsten." Pa Thor laughed a quick laugh. He rubbed his bristling chin. "Godalmighty, you never saw a gal like Kirsten. Thin as a willer, an' strong. Gettin' to the anxious age, too."

"Uhuh."

Pa Thor grinned and shook his head, seemingly amused with his own thoughts. "An' she sure kin get all stirred up about me. Gets me to work in the mornin' and hustles me all over the place. I'm kinda slow, I guess. Gettin' old. That's why I'm lookin' fer someone." He rubbed his leg.

Maury said nothing. He rummaged through his bundle until he found a spoon. He wiped it on his overall trousers until it shone and then tasted his beans. They were warm now. He pushed his cigarette stub into the dust to smother it. He nibbled at the beans slowly, chewing each one carefully to make the food last the length of a full meal.

21

The wind fell. It became very quiet, so quiet that the very stillness suggested the sound of silence. A stone rattled and squirreled down the side of the gully, clinked against the side of a tin can. There was a whisper of wind, then a sigh, then a pause, and then a heartbeat of earth.

Maury lifted his head. He held himself stiffly for a long minute, then relaxed. "Thought I heard a woman singin', but it musta been somethin' else."

Pa Thor said, puffing at his cigarette, "That was Kirsten. She sings pretty good. Danged if I don't like it, too."

"Yeah, some a them kin, all right."

Pa Thor watched him eat for a while and then said, "It's none a my business, but I can't figger out why a young bull of a man like you ain't lookin' fer work."

Maury's lips thinned. He suppressed an impulse to be rough.

Pa Thor sifted dust through his fingers as he rocked on his heels. "Take Kirsten. She's willin' to work on the farm. An' if she's willin' to stick out here, why! I think that should be good enough fer anybody."

Maury chewed slowly, watching the other sharply. "Matter of opinion, maybe."

"Huh! Wait till you see her, son."

Maury grunted.

"You know, son, I'd say you was makin' a mistake not stayin'. Even since the rain, there's been a change in the people hereabouts. Why! the storekeepers down at Sweet Grass are givin' credit again. It's a fact!"

Maury lifted the skillet from the fire and shook the beans to one side. Then he took a spoonful. He growled a little through the food as he talked. "Damn fools! Shucks, in a couple a weeks they'll know better. The greens'll all be as dead as dust again. Just watch."

"Think so?" Pa Thor rubbed his leg.

"I know so."

Maury noticed that every time Pa Thor began to lose an argument, he rubbed his leg.

Pa Thor cleared his throat, hawked, and spat into the fire. "Well, I dunno now. I know a man can be fooled by his own feelings. But, by God, I know that this spring I sure got a strong partic'ler feelin' that this summer we're goin' to have different weather."

"Huh!"

"Really! I can feel it. An' what's more, the people around Sweet Grass er feelin' the same thing. When people start laughin' at little ord'nary jokes they're feelin' better. An' that's . . ."

"Hell," Maury broke in. "Hell, they're not laughin' at the little jokes. They're just laughin' because they're nervous. Scared."

Pa Thor took a last puff from his cigarette and put it out beneath his shoe. Finally he filled his hand with dust again, closed his fingers gradually and tightly until little streams of the dust squirted out. "An' there's another thing. A course the young ones are so full of ginger they'd hitch their overalls and skirts at a fun'ral. But this spring they've been scratchin' theirselves uncommonly. They're pickin' each other fer keeps. An' some a the pa's and ma's I've seen in Sweet Grass are urgin' 'em on. That looks good to me."

Maury set his skillet on the fire again. There were a few beans left. He cleared his throat and shook his spoon at Pa Thor. "You know, hikin' along the road, a man gets to see things. An' I been watchin' the cattle an' horses." He looked at Pa Thor minutely. "Betcha yur cattle have fattened a little the last couple a weeks, ain't they?"

Pa Thor nodded solemnly.

"Sure, there you go. But they got light meat and they're full a bubbly fat, hain't they? Sure. An' there's milk in their tits, but the milk is goddam thin, ain't it? An' you're watchin' the milk like hawks, catchin' ev'ry drop and churnin' it fer cream an' cheese, ain't y'u?"

Pa Thor looked at him and then returned to watching his fingers play in the dust. "But they're slick and nice lookin' again."

Maury waved the argument aside with his hand. The beans were sizzling and he lifted them off the fire. "I know an' you know that the slickness is only temp'rary. Look. When you kin show me that the pheasants and coyotes and jackrabbits, and the birds and the bunnies, can make a livin' here, then I'll lissen to you." Then he muttered, "The prairie ain't no country atall without them cottontails."

Pa Thor nodded. He rubbed his leg vigorously. He pawed at his hat and then shoved it back on his neck. The sharp fire lighted the shadows in his wrinkles and his gray hair gleamed with silver.

Cold air fell from the sky. It tumbled on the warm ground, swirling and twirling in isolated gullies and valleys. There were little breathy winds. The warm air rushed upward. Stronger gusts spurted over the hills. Floating dust and newly ripped-up gray dust rode high. The gate squeaked in the wind.

Pa Thor stirred. "You don't want the bed, then?"

Maury looked over his shoulder at the shack. "No. Thanks."

Pa Thor stood up. "Well, I offered it to y'u."

Maury shrugged.

"Where did you say you was from?"

"Oklahoma."

"Kin still there?"

"No. They're gone."

24

"Californier?"

"No. Dead."

"Oh." Pa Thor pulled his hat over his forehead and then pushed it back again to scratch. "That's too bad, son. Hate to hear it."

Maury sat still, staring at the fire.

The old man's eyes relaxed. "Well . . . well . . . how come you come way up here?"

Maury cleared his throat. He squinted. He rubbed his knee. Then suddenly he poured it out. "Oh, well. Back in Oklahoma, when I was a kid, I saw how the grain hands was always goin' up north. After the grain was in, they'd work north through Kansas, Nebraska, Iowa, and then through the Dakotas, and on into Canada. An' so, when we was dusted out, I thought I'd follow their tail around a li'l. See if I could make a livin' the same way." He paused. "But, hell, Dakota turned out to be just as bad. If not worse."

"You an I.W.W.?"

"Nope. But I did join a union once. In the Omaha stockyards. It saved my neck fer a winter. But finally times got so bad not even the union could save my job. The bosses and the union had work only fer local men, not fer movers."

The old man nodded. "Uhuh. So. So y'u say your kin's dead, huh? All of 'em?"

"Just like I said."

Pa Thor sat down again. "Well, son, that's different. Way different."

"What's different?"

"That's way different. I didn't know that. I'm beginnin' to see, now, how it's been with you. Kin all dead an' gone. I'm beginnin' to see."

"See what?" Maury demanded.

"See what makes you go runnin' around like this.

Like a lost dog." Then, "Son, you ought to get yourself another fambly. A home. A place to live. Some people to care fer."

"Naw," said Maury gruffly. "No. I'm gettin' along all right. Don't worry about me."

"No, really, son. You ought to get yourself some people again. Really. It's very bad to go around without some people. When my Pa and Ma died, I went out an' got me my Thelma there, Ma Thor. Started up a new fambly right away. An' I ain't been sorry since."

Maury shook his head. He looked at the fire.

Above the low moan of the wind in the hollow steel posts, he heard the purr of a motor. Headlights picked out the house and the fringe of the gully.

Maury stood up. "That guy's got lights! Look. It's lit up here like a fair ground."

"Yeh."

Maury picked up his bundles, hastily jamming his spoon in his pocket. He clambered up the side of the roadbank.

"Where you goin', son?"

"Catch a ride, if I kin!" Maury faced the lights, his eyes blinking. He mustered a smile and waved. As the car slowed for the turn, he yelled, "Ride, mister?"

But the car zoomed on.

Maury watched the red tail light become smaller. Dust blurred it soon. He watched the headlights flicker over the fields. In the dancing lights, the bare arms of the creek willows clutched wildly at the sky. There was a smell of burnt oil.

"Not much luck," Pa Thor offered, as Maury settled down again and pulled out his spoon.

"No. Oh well, it's my own damned fault. Other times I ride the rails. But this time I had to be a wise guy. I thought I'd take a short-cut straight across this goddamn hell-country to Long Hope, an' catch the night freight there."

"Now, now, son. I just got through tellin' you the country ain't that bad," said Pa Thor slowly.

Maury ignored the remark. He asked, "Say, what time does that night freight run through Long Hope?"

"Oh . . . let's see. Two in the mornin'. Where you headin' fer?"

"The Black Hills. Heard they's hirin' fellas fer them gold mines there."

Pa Thor shook his head. "I wouldn't know about that."

"Say, how fer's them Bad Lands from here?"

"Oh, about twenty miles. Ever seen 'em?"

"No."

Pa Thor stared at the fire. Then he stirred and his eyes became dreamy with story. "You know, it's funny about this here country. Some people can live here all their life, an' yet be full a hate fer it. But not me. I love it. I love this land here, an' I love the Bad Lands. I go there sometimes just to look at 'em. Them purple spires have been a comfort to me many a time."

"Huh."

"Really, son. They're wonderful. Some time when you get a chance, take a good look at 'em. They're full a mystery." He sighed. "A course it's foolish to talk to other people about it. Foolish." Then, "An' yit, I hate to hoard all that earth-talk to myself, too."

Maury looked at the old man quizzically.

"An' then, there's the hills around here. There's Cedar Butte, an' Big Foot Hill. Both west a here. An' there's Eagles' Nest Butte which you kin see south a here on a clear day. Them's three nice hills, if you know how to look at them."

Again Maury looked up to study the old man.

Pa Thor scratched an ear. "Son, this land is full a history. Why! every spring some perfessors come up from the University to look it over. An' they always find new sets a old bones. The bones a nightmare critters. Dinosaurs they call 'em. It's wonderful." Then, "It's a wild land. A hard land. Ol' Gen'l Custer was sure right when he said it was hell with the fires burned out."

A phrase in Pa Thor's speech strummed a live chord in Maury's memory. He caught at it. "Nightmare critters, huh? That reminds me. I was hearin' in a little town back there," he gestured with his hand, "where them goddamn perfessors had dug up a batch of them there dinosaur eggs an' let 'em lay in the sun, an' they hatched, an' now this country is crawlin' with nightmare snakes, horrible things, spittin' and chewin' up the people."

Pa Thor jumped. "Why, that's ridiculous! That's the kind a talk that always pops up when ignorunt people get together and chew the rag. Always. 'Specially when they's lost their head. When they get silly in the head."

Maury shrugged. "Huh, it's probably because they get too hungry. Hungry people get funny notions. I do."

"Poppycock! It don't come from no hunger. It comes from ignorunt people who don't know no better."

Again Maury shrugged.

"No, son, they're wrong. Because this is a wonderful country. It's a little hard, but it's wonderful."

"Huh."

Suddenly Pa Thor stood up with a guilty look in his eye. "By gosh, I plumb forgot. My wimminfolks'll wonder what happened to me. Guess I better turn in." He paused a moment before he started up the side of the gully. "Sure you don't want a bed?"

"No. This'll be all right. Besides, if a car comes along, I want to catch it. Thanks."

28

"Well, if you're still settin' here in the mornin', why just drop aroun' fer a cup a fresh coffee. Still got some milk, an' a cup a coffee's a nice thing in the mornin'." The old man went up the side of the gully. Then he turned to look down at Maury once more. And all the while he searched through his pockets for a pouch of tobacco, filled his pipe and lighted it, he stood on the edge of the gully, studying Maury. When he had his pipe going, he walked away into the dark.

"Funny ol' coot," Maury muttered, as he turned to his beans again. "Talkative old nut. Been talkin' to himself all these years, an' now he's gotta hear himself talk no matter who's aroun'." He punched his spoon in the skillet. "He should have a dog." Then, "Kind a nice, though. Got a good heart like my Pa." He looked at the fire for a long while, thinking. Then he shrugged. "Well, that's all dead an' past now. Got to look ahead. Golly, I sure wish I could get my fingers on a job soon."

Later he again heard footsteps padding on the ground above. They were softer than Pa Thor's.

Maury became exasperated. He growled a rough, "Howdy," then said, "Well, c'mon down." He grumbled to himself. "This hole's gettin' to be a regular depot, people comin' an' goin' through it like it was public." He refused to look up. "Every damn day I gotta feed some . . . some poor little critter comin' along. Christ."

The footsteps halted above him. He looked up. This time it was a girl. "Whew!" he suddenly whistled, looking at her light-brown hair. "Whew!" Involuntarily, he stood up and touched his cap. He stared at her blue eyes and her slim, overalled figure. She was tall, leanly muscled, and tanned a gold-brown. Her overalls were large enough to be her father's. "I ain't got much left," Maury began, "but . . ."

29

The girl clambered down the bank easily. "Go ahead an' finish your eatin'. Pa said there was a stranger sittin' in the gully here who turned down a night's rest in a bed, an' I was wonderin' just what kind a critter that could be."

Maury recovered. He drew himself up stiffly. "Well, this hain't a zoo!"

The girl laughed. Though her body was hard and wiry, she laughed very gently. Her voice rolled the words slightly, as if she might be a singer. It was pleasant to his ears. "Pa said you was a nice feller, and smart too. Looked just like my brother Tollef, he said. Just like him. If Tollef was alive, you'd be his dead-ringer twin, he said."

Maury considered this burst of talk. After a moment, he seized on an idea in it. "What happened to Tollef?"

"Died."

"How come?"

"Got lost in a dust storm. Choked to death."

"Huh. That's too bad."

"An' Pa said you was playin' a guitar. That's one thing Tollef couldn't do." Her eyes questioned him.

Maury nodded. "I was afraid your Pa'd heard me." He sat down on his heels again.

The girl settled on her heels too on the other side of the fire. "Play it some."

"No." Maury splintered a small board lying at his feet. He fed the fire with the small kindling he had made. Then he looked up. "You Kirsten?"

"Yes."

"Thought so." He studied her. "You sure your Pa didn't tell you I was a no-good bindlestiff, with an eye on your chicken coop?"

"No. Pa said you looked all right to him. Said you looked just like Tollef. Said you was his dead-ringer."

She paused, looking into the fire again. "He kept sayin' it."

Maury looked at her with suspicion in his eyes. He had a sudden idea that the old man had sent her down to see him for a purpose. "What kind a game you people playin' with me?"

"No game. We ain't playin' no game."

Maury grunted. "Well, it's all right." He muttered to himself as he finished his beans. Presently, he asked, "Name a Thor is Scandy, ain't it?"

Kirsten nodded.

"Church people?"

"We was. But the church is gone now. Why?"

"Oh, you sounded like it, like some a them meddlin', missionary kind. Preachin', soul-savin', with a gospel message."

"Oh, no, we're not that kind."

"Huh! Once a christer, always a christer. Hell, we had some a them down in Oklahoma. Prayed all summer and winter fer a little rain. Prayed an' prayed. Maybe they're still prayin' fer all I know. They never caught on that the good Lord had left the land. Never caught on. Dumb bastards."

Kirsten drew herself up with obvious distaste. Her lips thinned.

Maury wiped his mouth and ran his tongue along the edges of his lips. He noticed her stiffness. "Don't act like a sassiety dame that's sat on her hatpin, kid."

Kirsten still sat stiffly.

A car approached. The light swept above them against the house. Maury jumped up, grabbed his two bundles, and scaled the side of the gully part way. Then he threw out his arm and shouted urgently, "Ride, mister?"

But the car skittered around the corner. A little fusillade of gravel sprayed into the gully. A puff of dust

31

soared in a circle above them and then drifted down.

Maury thumbed his nose energetically.

Kirsten said reprovingly, "You shouldn't do that."

"Well, as far as I'm concerned, they kin," Maury said, settling before the fire again, "Anyway, what's it to you?"

"Nobody owes you a ride."

Grumbling as if he thought all this talk a waste of breath, Maury picked up the skillet again, inspected it, and then wiped the inside of it with a long finger. He looked into the empty bean can and then threw it over his shoulder. It clanked amongst the other metal junk. He wiped the spoon on his overalls and carefully put it away in his bundle.

"Well, don't sit there like a mummy," he said finally, as he rolled and lighted another cigarette. He squinted at her with sharp eyes. She was a very becoming girl, he decided reluctantly. He wiggled his fingers. "If you're gonna stick around, woman, talk up."

She was silent.

"Well, okay. Don't say nothin' then. I suppose you're tryin' to impress me you're one a them clean country gals? Well, don't tell me!" He snorted. "I lived in the country. An' I know. The country gals'll lay in the grass as soon as the city dames will."

Kirsten ignored the talk. She sat looking at the ground. Her hair had fallen, hiding her face from him. Through the V of her shirt front, he could see the upper slopes of her full breasts.

"Well, it's all right, Kir . . . kid. It's all right."

She looked at him. "You kin call me Kirsten if you want."

Maury puffed at his cigarette and measured her. "As I was sayin', it's all right. I've been runnin' aroun' the country fer a long time now, an' I've found out that everybody's got somethin' to hide. Everybody."

The gate creaked above. The burlap in the barn window fluttered with short popping sounds. Dust drifted over them. A hollow steel fence post moaned.

Maury rolled over on his side, facing his guitar. He ran his fingers over the edges. "Your Pa tells me you kin sing?"

Kirsten nodded.

"Did y'u ever have a fella?"

Kirsten was slow answering.

"Did y'u?" he asked, grinning at her slyly.

"Once," she said finally.

"Bad?"

She said nothing. She stared at the fire.

He studied her. He wondered what mysterious pictures were alive in her mind now. Perhaps she was seeing again the calf-like face of some local farm boy, clumsily putting his arm over her. He asked suddenly, "Did you shake him?"

She nodded.

Maury scratched and cleaned his nose vigorously for a moment. "Well, kid . . . Kirsten, you needn't worry about me. I ain't got time fer such as you. You're different, I guess. You're not the quick-just-a-minute kind. An' I ain't got time except fer such as those."

"Ain't got time?"

"No. No, I hain't." And Maury stirred on his heels. "No, I got to hurry. I got to get on to the Hills an' get hired before they quit takin' any more men at the gold mines. Got to lay up a little dough so's I kin set out fer myself. I . . . well, the way I see it, though it's nice fer a man to be workin', he's got to be free, too."

"Wouldn't you be free on a farm?"

"Naw, farmin's too much a gamble. Why! woman, I saw how my Pa worked himself to the bone on his farm. An' he died in debt." He paused. "It's all right to be born in debt, that's good fer a man. Makes him agitate to get somewhere. But when he dies in debt after a lifetime a turrible work, that's not right. That's not right atall. Naw, farmin's not fer me. Not out here, anyway."

"Well, we're still here."

"And how! You're damn near starved, too!"

Kirsten picked up a small piece of wood and fed it to the fire. "Well, I know it's bad out here, all right." She paused. Then, "Pa said you was a farm boy once and that your Pa an' Ma died. But I didn't know you felt that way about it."

Maury grunted. "Huh! Woman, don't try to talk to me about farmin'. You'll waste your breath." He lay down in the dust, half-facing the dying embers. He scratched his back and then his arms. He looked at his fingers closely and pulled out the tumbleweed pricks he had picked up when he had crushed the weeds for kindling. He mumbled, half to himself. "This damned pricky stuff! What a helluva dump! Boy, the hair on Uncle Sam's bread basket is sure pretty skimpy right now." He laughed a little at his own joke, and waited for an answering chuckle from her. But when he saw that Kirsten was off by herself, studying the fire, he looked down at his fingers again, picking at the thorns. Presently he put his hand under his head and pushed his elbow into the dust. He rested. He looked at the drifting dust above.

The steel post cried. The gate swung sometimes, its creak rising slowly and then snapping silent with a sharp crunch.

Maury mused aloud. "Christ, I'll bet the crows have to carry their own grub across this country. Dust, dust, dust. By God, Kirsten, how can you people stand it?"

"Well, where else could we go?"

"Oh, somewhere."

"That where you've been since you left home?"

Maury's face clouded. Then, watching her face, he asked, "I suppose you think I'm a bum?"

"Oh no. Like Pa said, you look like Tollef."

He laughed.

"No, really, you look all right to me." Then, "At least, there's nothin' wrong with you that a little work on a farm wouldn't cure."

"Huh! Don't fool yourself." He paused. "Woman, take a good look at me. Don't I look like a bindlestiff? A wand'rin' bastard from hell itself? Kirsten, let me tell you something. I'm a bum, really. And there's a lot more like me. Millions. Just driftin' aroun' like this dust and these tumbleweeds here, with no place to stick fer a spell. Just a bunch a shaggy weasels tryin' to find a hole." He thought a moment, then shrugged. "Well, anyway, it's better to be a drifter, an' on your own, than to be a reliefer . . . which I'd a been if I'd a stayed there in that hole in Oklahoma."

Kirsten rubbed her leg slowly. She shook her head. "No, no. No, I don't think so. Look at us. We're not on relief."

"Yeh, but you sure could use some." He paused to rub his nose, then he smiled a little embarrassedly as a thought came to him. "I guess it hain't polite to point." He drew in a quick breath. "Well, let's look at me then. Sure, I had a few dinky jobs the last four years. But, I always felt like I was dust under somebody's heel. An' a farm boy can't stand that. He's been brought up independent." He paused and turned over on his back to look at the faint stars. "One time a fella I know let me run his hamburger joint. He was sick that day an' he tol' me to run it an' take all the proceeds fer the day. All the day's profit was mine, see. I never had so much fun in all my life." He hesitated. "I was independent, I was."

"Yes. As independent as a hog on ice," Kirsten observed.

Maury started, and then laughed. "Woman, you sure got a sharp tongue." He squinted. "Well, maybe you're right, at that." He scratched his hip and crossed his legs. Then he sat up and loosened his shoes. He took them off, smelled them, made a wry face, and then drew off his socks. He pushed his feet luxuriously through the soft dust. Then he lay back again, scratching his hip. "Well, so, I've come to the conclusion that this me here is just a miscue in a game a snooker. I suppose that even if I do get a job there in the Hills, an' start rollin' in the dough, an' savin' it, I'll still be tied down. An' God, I want to be free. As free as the wind."

"An' as hungry?"

Maury waited a moment and then laughed hollowly. "Guess you got me there again, kid." Then he exclaimed, "By golly, Kirsten, hard times sure sharpened your tongue!"

Kirsten smiled, and then asked, "Why don't you play your guitar once?"

Quickly Maury drew up his guard. "Naw, I never play fer others. Never. It's a rule." Then, "Besides, I don't play so good."

"Pa says you do. Real good. Says you sound like a professional. Play some."

"Woman, compliments don't work on me. Why! there's been times when God's called on me to play, an' I've refused."

She looked at him, laughing a little.

"S'fact!"

"Aw, play some," she begged.

"Listen, woman. I play fer nobody but myself. Hear?"

Kirsten quailed a little then.

Maury went on after a moment. "I didn't mean to bite

36

you. But, I'm not myself these days. Worried. Too worried. I'm tryin' to figure out a way to make a decent livin'." He paused. "An', I've been tryin' to figure out why I'm livin'. Did y'u ever do that? I've done a lot of it. I've done it because I wanted to know where I was goin'. An', because I'd like to do somethin' I really like. You know, somethin' that'd hum in me all day long an' make me go to work in the mornin' whistlin', a jinglin' a little free chickenfeed in my pockets . . . why! woman, that'd be the real life!"

She nodded.

He said, "Y'u know, a guy hates to crawl to work he hates. Where they beat the guts out a him all day long an' whip a blacksnake at him in his dreams at night." His eyelids were drawn thin. He sighed. Then he grinned a little at her. "Well, kid, here I've been talkin' about me all the time. Let's talk about you. You're sure a nice clean girl to be growin' up out here with no man to see you. It's kind of a waste."

Kirsten looked up apprehensively.

Maury saw her indrawn eyes. He pretended to drop his interest in her. He looked at the slow fire. He mused on it and played with his toes in the dust. "Funny, that about your Pa. Kept invitin' me in. He sounded just like Billy Sunday invitin' me into heaven."

"Well, it's like Pa says. We always got coffee and cot fer wandering farm boys."

"Well, that's mighty accommodatin'." He sidled closer to her, watching her hands rub her legs. He watched her covertly. " 'Specially since maybe you people'd be on the road yourself before long, and'd be wantin' some coffee an' kindness too."

"Huh! Not us!"

Maury put his arm over her shoulder. He hung it awkwardly on her stiff, tense body. "By God, you people sure got it bad. It reminds me of this mornin' . . ." He placed his hand on her breast. Still she sat stiffly. "As I was sayin', it reminds me of this mornin'. I was sittin' in a fillin' station, waitin' fer a ride." He moved his hand to her lap. Her fingers were white on her legs now. "I counted fifty-two men, ten women, an' fourteen kids thumbin' rides. Station guy there said they just keep comin' on, hundreds a them every day, like tumbleweeds in the fall." Maury lifted his hand from her lap to wave it back and forth a few times. Then he replaced it. "They kept lookin', lookin', lookin'. An' what got me, was that them people could always snap on a smile when a car came along. They might be down, but they had enough left to turn on the light-switch."

"What about it?" she asked coldly, trying to drop his arm by straightening her body.

But he drew his arm about her more intimately. "Well, it's just like you folks. You keep hangin' on even when you're licked. I like that. You got guts."

Kirsten moved suddenly. She threw his hand aside. She slapped him hard. "You got guts too, mister!"

"Aw, now," Maury murmured. He tried to restrain her.

But she leaped free of his reach.

Maury looked at her admiringly. "By golly, I guess you're all right at that!"

She started up the incline.

Maury watched her. "Woman, I told you everybody has an axe to grind. I can't help it if I get to reachin' fer a nice lookin' girl like you." He squinted at her, wondering if she would turn for one last word. When she did not respond, he dismissed her with a wave of his hand.

In a moment, he heard the door of the shack slam.

The wind died down.

Maury looked at the fire a moment, and then, kneeling before it, opened the second bag. Fondly, he picked over the objects in it. There was an old straight razor, an almost-bald shaving brush marked with worn gold initials, M.G., a pencil, a notebook filled with irregularly scribbled addresses, miniature pictures of his mother and father carefully wrapped in an empty billfold, a torn Bible, and a sheaf of old newspapers. He fumbled with these things nostalgically. Then, snapping his eyes, he rearranged his possessions carefully and, except for the newspapers, wrapped them all together again. His restless eyes were soft.

He extinguished the fire with a few handfuls of dust. He settled on a dust-drift, drawing the newspapers carefully over his body as though they were sheets on a bed. He arranged his bundle beneath his head for a pillow. Then he drew his guitar bundle close against his body. He nuzzled his hard pillow a few times.

There was a smell of grass and weeds on the rising wind. A train hooted and rumbled in the distance. A falling meteor gashed the sky. The earth seemed to rise up through the bustle of the wind, rise toward a black sky full of white stars. The earth and the sky came close together. The gate creaked. The hollow steel post talked. An awakened rooster crowed behind the shack. A stone rolled down the side of the gully. Maury slept.

III

BEFORE MAURY WOKE, a thin sliver of gray pried the earth and the sky apart. Stars faded immediately above the creeping light.

Roosters in the Thor chicken coop were already crowing when the earth slipped like an immense gray potato from a lifting forkful of blackness. The earth and the sky parted. The sky became blue-black, then blue, then burst with quick light. The earth changed from gray to dark green-black, then green-gray. Yellow haloes limned the buildings and knolls.

Dew had fallen in the night, emphasizing the color of the germinal growths in the small valleys and lowlands, the pasture and hay land and grainfields, deepening the growths into a quick green. For a moment the gray patches of exposed soil were black with suggestive richness.

Maury was still sleeping when the night's coolness began to vanish. He was clumsily comfortable in the dust-drift on the bottom of the gully. His shoulder was deep in the powder, and a sprinkling of it on his hair was like silver. He snored heavily, his mouth barely parted and drooling; and below it lay a spot of black mud where his saliva had intermittently dropped in the dust. Spittle-balls had rolled themselves into thin blankets of dust and had run down the incline of the drift like grand-daddy spiders.

A wind scuffed at the edge of the gully and dinged the gate.

A murmur of words stirred the Thor house. Once there was a sharp spurt of words. In a moment, Kirsten came out of the door and looked sleepily at the sun.

Pa Thor followed her, carrying two clanking milk pails. As he turned toward the barn, he stopped and talked to her.

Kirsten nodded. She brushed back her hair and looked at the sun again. She stretched. She yawned. She tightened a suspender on her overall. She sat down and slowly pulled on her shoes. Then she walked toward the gully.

Maury stirred a little. Sleep had erased the squint and his mouth was thinly red and unwrinkled. When Kirsten scuttled down the side of the gully, the noise of falling dirt awakened him. He sat up quickly.

"Good mornin'. We thought maybe you'd like some coffee," she said, smiling briefly.

Maury looked at her with reddened eyes. He was puzzled for a moment. Then he remembered. "Oh, howdy. Huh! I thought I'd never set eyes on you again."

"Well, it ain't my doin'. Pa said I was to offer you some coffee."

Maury's eyes formed their squint again. He grunted and rubbed his eyes. He yawned. "Well, I guess it won't hurt to take a little bit a coffee, at that."

He stood up then, drew on his shoes, and folded his newspapers carefully. He opened a bundle and shoved them inside. Then, picking up the two bundles in his left hand, he walked up the side of the gully with her.

At the top, he stood still a moment, watching the first anger of the morning sun. He stretched and yawned again, involuntarily. He sighed deeply. He snapped his right hand against his trousers to shake out the dust. A morning wind caught the dust and fluttered it over the edge of the gully. Then he turned and walked silently with Kirsten toward the house.

Another breath of morning wind came up. He saw it scuffle in the dust on a bare patch of ground before the house. A miniature cloud of dust tumbled a few inches along a serried dust dune and then vanished. Sometimes the gray flour eddied around a clod, whispering around to the left and then to the right. First the dust lay quiet, then it stirred, and then, mysteriously, it lay quiet again.

"If you'll pump some water from the well, I'll get the washpan and the soap so's you kin wash up a bit," she offered.

Maury nodded. He placed the bundles on a bench near the steps of the house and started across the yard with a pail. Tufts of burnt grass spotted the ground. The yard was as bare as a worn fur rug.

Maury hung the pail on the pump nose. He jerked the handle up and down a few times, and then realized that the well was almost dry. He pumped rapidly until he felt the suction rubber grab deep in the earth. A few more strokes brought yellow-gray water to the surface and it splashed in the pail. He pumped until the pail was full. Then he set it to one side, and, holding his hand over the spout, drank slowly while his other hand moved the handle with deliberate strokes.

Before he picked up the pail, he stood looking at the country. The open fields rolled away over small hummocks and knolls. He could see deserted farms in the distance.

"God, it's quiet out here," he muttered, as he rolled a cigarette. He licked the side of it and then, feeling that his mouth was dry inside, turned his tongue against the roof of his mouth, spreading moisture with a smacking noise. He searched in his pocket for a match. Lighting his cigarette, he turned to listen again to the morning sounds. "It's damn dead here," he said, "damn dead. Not a damn thing stirrin' yet. No trucks rollin', or wind cryin' or crickets sawin' or frogs blowin' out their bellies, or turtledoves honin' out their hearts in the willers.

When a country don't get no rain, it's worse'n bein' dead. God, how I'd hate to live here. Just go nuts, I would."

He looked at the trees along the creek and north of the house. A few of the branches had sprouted leaves, but these already hung limply. He shook his head.

"You don't like it, huh?"

Maury turned, to see Kirsten beside him. "Naw," he said, picking up the pail. "No. Nothin's movin' here. I was just lookin' at the trees there. I remember down in Oklahoma, when I was a kid, the trees would be full a song in the mornin', robins an' jays an' cacklin' sparrows. Now just look at them there trees. Nothin' in 'em. Just nothin'. An' lissen to the damn ol' earth. It ain't talkin' like it should. Why! a man should be hearin' the roosters crowin' an' pigs gruntin' an' milk pails clankin', an' menfolks callin' the horses an' cows an' pigs." He paused a moment. "An' a man should be seein' the bunny little cottontails flaggin' in the brush."

Kirsten took the pail out of his hands and said quietly, "But you will. Just you wait."

He swept his eyes over the flat, desolate prairie again. His eyes alighted on the old windmill frame. "That yours? That junkpile a bones?"

She nodded. "The wind took it down last fall. An' Pa can't get help to set it up."

He looked around again. "Funny, I don't see a windmill anywhere. Or buildings. What happened?"

"The wind blew 'em all down."

He looked at the shack and the barn and the privy and the toolshed. "That's funny. Them buildings ain't strong. How come they didn't go, too?"

"That's probably because God respected the people who stayed livin' here."

"Huh!" he snorted contemptuously. "What a country! The only thing still livin' is the highway and the railway an' the telephone wires. An' they have to reach in from the outside or they'd die too." He paused and stared at a distant building. "What's that?"

"Consolidated country school."

"Ain't no kids fer it, is there?"

"No. But the school's real nice. Guv'ment keeps it painted."

He shrugged his shoulders. "Huh! They're wastin' their time."

Maury puffed at his cigarette and then started toward the house with her. As they came to the steps, he looked at her curiously. "Christ! You people must be plumb nuts!"

Kirsten poured the water into the wash basin.

Maury tossed away his cigarette, opened his shirt, and rolled up his sleeves.

Then a mellow voice asked, "He stayin' fer breakfast?"

Maury looked up. "Howdy," he greeted. He saw a friendly, heavy-set woman. She had kind eyes and a firm, thin mouth. Her hands were big and red. "Good mornin' to you, Ma'am."

"Good mornin'," Ma Thor said. He could feel her making an estimate of him as she raised her eyes slowly from his feet to his head. Then she looked quickly at Kirsten. "You tol' him we ain't got much?"

Kirsten smiled. "He don't need to be told. He knows. He's been grumbling about this country already."

"Oh," said Ma Thor. She held her eyes on his soaped face for a moment and then turned and walked into the house. Maury watched her square hips rise and fall into the darkness of the interior.

"You got a nice Ma there," Maury said after a moment, as he rinsed the soap from his face. He waited for an answer. Then he asked, "Where's your Pa?"

"He's milkin' the cows."

"Got a calf?"

"No. Pa feeds a little of the milk to the sow."

"Don't leave much for you folks, does it?"

"No."

Maury rubbed his fingers briskly. "Both cows bred again?"

"No. We've been tryin' to find a neighbor with a bull. But there ain't any."

Maury shook his head. "Well, guess I can't help much there."

Kirsten grimaced wryly.

Maury watched her and laughed.

"Here comes Pa," she said. "He's stayin' fer breakfast," she announced.

Pa Thor came up. "Good. That's good." He hesitated on the steps. He looked around at the open fields. "Well, what do you think of her?"

Maury said dryly, "Well, it's a nice country, but you need water."

"Oh, we'll get some," Pa Thor said hopefully. "I felt my leg actin' up again this mornin'. An' it's one a the best weather vanes in the country. Never fails. An' right now it seems to be achin' around fer a change in the weather." He looked at the sky for a sign of a cloud. "I'm almost sure we'll get a change tonight. Ache is pretty strong."

Maury grunted as he dried his face on an old towel. "Well, I've been achin' fer four years now, every bone in me, an' if each ache had meant a cloud the world would've washed away by now."

Pa Thor stilled. He settled on his heels on the steps.

Kirsten sat down beside him.

Then, presently, Pa Thor stirred again. He coughed, and said, "Well, the dew always helps a little, though.

45

Freshens up the greens some."

"Yeh, an' helps fry 'em better when the sun gets high."

"Well . . . it'll be all right. Some day, when the rains come again, the land will turn green an' lift into the hills, an' roll again. I know it will." He looked dreamily over the land. "That'll sure be nice, when she cracks with growin' things. It sure will. There'll be bright greens, an' chickens peckin' away under the tall grain. Why! we're liable to have a bumper any year now!"

Maury murmured disgustedly to himself. He waited for Pa Thor to get up to wash and then took the old man's place on the steps beside Kirsten. He fumbled with his cigarette makings.

They were silent together. There was only the noise of Pa Thor splashing his face with water. Kirsten sat as still as a watchful creature.

Soon Ma Thor came to the door. "You kin come in now," she said.

They filed in slowly.

Maury looked quickly around. The house reminded him of his home. There, in the back to the north, was the room where the family slept. Its door opened near the wall. Here, in the kitchen, they were assembling about the table against the south wall. A black stove with nickel trimmings stood against the center of the west wall. A window opened on either side of it, and he could see the fields stretching away to the rim of the earth. An old, well-oiled shotgun hung over the stove beneath the worm-elbow of the stovepipe. A dish cabinet and a cooking work-table stood against the east wall. There was a window in the center of the wall. The curtains were gray and frayed and much washed. There was an atmosphere of neatness about. Maury's face lighted a little. When he turned to the table, he saw that Kirsten had been watching him. He smiled briefly.

46

Ma Thor said, "Mister, you take that chair there, across from Kirsten. Pa, pull up your chair from the winder."

Pa Thor groaned a little as he pulled the chair across the room. "My leg does ache a little harder this mornin'."

"Sure, Pa. Sure. That's good," Ma Thor said, comfortingly.

Pa Thor shifted in his creaking armchair and rubbed his leg.

Ma Thor pushed the plates around with little nervous gestures. "We ain't got much. We just got some tapioca an' some bread an' coffee. Used to have some bacon, but . . ."

"Oh, that's all right," Maury said, sliding a portion of tapioca onto his plate. "This looks plenty good to me."

There was a brisk smell of coffee in the room. After a moment, Maury felt comfortable. He expanded a little. "Sure nice a you folks. Takin' in a stranger like me. Pretty nice. Very." Then he added hastily, " 'Course, I know how farm folks is. They're all friendly. My folks was too."

Ma Thor asked, "How long since you left the farm?"

"Four years ago. Four years." He looked at his plate. "Golly, that's a long time to be nowheres at all! Golly! An' I ain't done nothin' since. If this keeps up I won't have nothin' to look forward to, or nothin' to look backward at."

Pa Thor hitched his chair closer. "Son, are you pretty broke?"

"Yeh." Then after a few ticks of silence, he added, "Yes. Pretty broke."

Pa Thor went on, craftily, "You know, you act like you think it ain't gonna rain in this country again."

Maury looked at him directly. "Well, to tell you the truth, I don't think it is."

47

Pa Thor nodded. "Well, 'course my leg could just be kickin' up a little. Anyway, that crick a mine is still runnin' with water. And all of it is slippin' away an' doin' no good. I was thinkin' it over yestiddy, an' figgered that if it wasn't gonna rain no more it might not be such a bad idea to build a little dam down there where she turns by the willers. Nice little spot there fer a dam. It'd soak up the ground on the lower forty, an' if a man took some time an'd run the water along little ditches, why! a man might get a few bushels a grain and corn."

Maury rolled a lump of food over in his mouth. He visualized the idea, then said, "Well, now, that sounds pretty good." He chewed the food and swallowed it. "You know, it's a cinch it won't rain any more. Danged if that ain't a hell of an idea."

Pa Thor pulled his chair closer. "Well, that's what I thought. An' my two hay-burners, Becky and Beaut, they've been eatin' pretty good these last few weeks, an' they kin stand a little work now. An' I got an old scraper. One a the handles ain't so good, but there's spare branches around that won't do no more growin'. But you see, I'm too old to hold down the danged scraper. The ground's too goldurn hard. It's like cement. An' Kirsten . . . by golly, I don't want my daughter to rip up her belly doin' it either. So you see how it is, son."

Ma Thor poured out some more coffee for Maury. She held the lid on the coffee pot with the corner of her apron spread over her fingers. She said, "If we had Tollef, but . . ." A few tears came into her eyes.

Maury knew what was coming. He felt uncomfortable. "Well, I dunno now."

Ma Thor went on, "This boy looks somewhat like him too, don't he?" she asked Kirsten wistfully.

Kirsten nodded.

48

Maury said suddenly, "Now look here. Damn it, i'm in a hurry to get to the Hills. Just gotta hurry to get out there. Just gotta. I've been wanderin' aroun' fer four years, four years a my best life. An' there's a chance, just a chance I kin lay up a little dough diggin' in the gold mines, an' then set out fer myself. An' if I stay here to help you, well, hell, probably the jobs will be all filled up."

Pa Thor reflected, "But if you've been out in the open so long, on the road an' on the farm, do you think you'll like the gold mines? Do you think you could live inside a dark, wet hole?"

Maury was stubborn. "Anyway, I can't stay here. I've been talkin' a workin' in the gold mines fer days now, an' ain't never got to it yit. Now that there's jobs there, I ought to go. I just gotta go on."

Pa Thor considered. "Well, we can sell a little of the cream. Maybe . . . do you think, Ma, Kirsten, do you think we kin pay him a little somethin' besides keep?"

Ma Thor said, "I dunno now. We got to get you a new overall. An' there's bakin' stuff to buy. Gotta think a that, too."

"I know."

Ma Thor said, and Maury could feel her looking at his shoulders and his grim mouth, "I think we can give him something, Pa."

Pa Thor studied the streaks of tapioca in his plate. "Well, son, suppose we give you a dollar fer three days' work. That'll just do it. We kin do the dam in three days, if there ain't no rain. An' if there's rain . . . why! then we'll pay more."

"No."

There was a silence in the room. Maury sat awkwardly at the table.

Ma Thor said, "Well, if the young feller don' wanna

. . . why, Pa, I s'pect you ought to let him go. He knows his own mind."

Maury said, feeling easier, "Well, I would help you, but you know, I gotta get started. I feel like I've been wastin' a lot a good time these last four years."

Pa Thor stood up tiredly. "Guess I better get to movin' on the yard. Kirsten, you gonna help me get the horses?"

Kirsten stood up and nodded. She looked at Maury silently, then followed Pa Thor through the door.

Maury stood up to go.

Ma Thor began to pile up the plates. "Pa feels bad about your not helpin' him. He's been trying to get some one out here fer a couple a weeks. But there just ain't nobody. Some a them bums in Sweet Grass got the time an' need the money, but they think the dam's a fool stunt. No, Pa's gonna feel bad, and Kirsten too."

"But you see how it is, Mrs. Thor."

Ma Thor nodded. "If the dam works, you could stay all year round, you know. Pa's thataway."

Maury said weakly, "I'd stay a couple a days. But . . . well, trouble is, you people'd figger I'd stay all year round. An' . . . Mrs. . . . Ma, I'd go nuts if I had to work here knowin' there was nothin' ahead 'cept starvin' and chokin' in the dust."

Ma Thor looked at him sharply. "What about us? An' Kirsten?"

Maury looked at his feet. He was standing in the open door and he could hear Pa Thor and Kirsten calling the horses. "I know it," he grumbled. He thought a moment, scratched his backsides, and then said, "Okay then. But the only way I'll help is knowin' that at any minute I kin quit . . . that I'm doin' it as a lark."

"Sure, son."

Maury scuffed his shoe on the doorsill. "Guess I better bring in my things then."

Ma Thor said, "I got a cot upstairs in the attic. It's Tollef's. I'll get it down and set it by the stove, there by the winder. An' you kin set your things there fer the time bein'."

Maury brought in his bundles and then went outside. He walked across the yard and then, hesitant, entered the barn.

Pa Thor, harnessing the horses, held his hands still and stared at him.

Kirsten straightened quickly.

Maury's eyes shifted to the ground. Then he said, "Well, c'mon. Get the harnesses on. The sun's et a big hole in the day already."

Pa Thor swallowed twice.

Kirsten brightened.

Maury looked at the harness, and then reached for the crupper. He slipped it under the tail. "Which one is Becky?" he asked.

Pa Thor said hastily, "This one. This spotted gray one. The straight gray is Beaut."

"Good horses," Maury commented, slapping Beaut's rump. "But they's a bit weak yit."

"Well, we'll work 'em easy, son."

Maury nodded. He slipped off the halter from Becky's head and replaced it with a bridle. Then he led her outdoors.

Kirsten had gone ahead. She was already pumping water into a cracked, wooden tank.

Looking at her, Maury asked, "Water 'em?"

Pa Thor nodded. "Know how to hitch horses?"

"Sure."

"Well, I have to get an axe an' some nails an' a hammer. May have to do a little buildin' to brace up the dirt."

Maury led the horses to the tank where Kirsten was

pumping, and watered them. His eyes kept straying to Kirsten's overalled figure. He was pleased with her brief smile. He muttered, "Well, I'm stayin', but just fer a day or two. That's all."

Kirsten nodded.

Maury saw Pa Thor listening to them as he stood before the toolshed door. When Maury stared directly at him, Pa Thor went hastily inside.

Presently, they were all walking together across the yard, and turning down the pasture lane, west toward the creek. Maury pointed to a deserted farm yard toward the south. "Where'd they go?"

"Usta be a churchful a Germans out there along the White River. But they's moved out. They was Lutherans. Funny, when things got bad, they all moved out the same time, moved out the whole shebang."

Maury nodded. "White River, huh?"

Pa Thor said, "Yeh. See them tops a trees an' rollin' hills out there? That's the White River. Danged near dry. Lot a alkali out there. Land's flaked white with it."

Then they were near the creek. Kirsten said, pointing to a bare country graveyard in the distance, "Pa's been wantin' to take out the stone an' plant a little something there, but Ma says that wouldn't be right. Says it's bad enough people can't live in peace when they're alive without someone stirrin' them up when they're dead."

Maury looked west toward the rolling hills. "That where the Bad Lands are?"

Pa Thor said, "Sure. An' if you'll look sharp, you kin see some a them spires I was tellin' you about last night. There's Cedar Butte. Can't quite see Big Foot Hill. But," and Pa turned to point south, "that thing that looks like a bit of cloud there, that's Eagles' Nest Butte."

Maury looked, and nodded. The vacant land stirred him. He asked, "Did many people die aroun' here?"

"Sure," said Pa Thor. "There was Ol' John. Tollef an' me was workin' by the crick one day an' I says, all of a sudden remembering, 'Say, Tollef, don't you smell somethin' dead?' He smells. An' I smells. An' sure, it stunk like somethin' dead all right. An' we walks over an' there was Ol' John. Croaked. Died dry. Just turned over on his side an' died alone."

"Christ!" Maury said softly.

Pa Thor said swiftly then, "Well, it'll rain soon now. And the hills'll be lifting again."

They reached the creek. Maury looked across the knoll on which they were standing.

And suddenly he became interested in the project. Most knolls in the land, he saw, were new dust dunes. But the knoll he was standing on and the other across the stream were naturally firm. And as this first knoll was the larger, it would be simple to cut it down with a scraper and keep working the dirt from it across the stream until they had reached the other knoll. The two knolls then would become anchors for the dam. The tramping and the weight of the heavy scraper would harden the new dirt as they went along. Yes, it would work. Reluctantly, he smiled.

"Well, son, what do you think, huh?"

"We kin do her, all right. An' we'll keep linin' her with branches and tumbleweeds as we go along, and tramp down what we do good an' tight."

Pa Thor nodded. "That's just what I thought. Well, when do we begin?"

"Any time you say, Pa." Then, looking once more over the land before beginning the work, he observed, "But before we start fillin' in the dam, I think we better fill in some a them cracks there."

Pa Thor looked up with a quick resentment, as though at uncalled-for slander. "Where? I didn't see any around here. They all closed up this spring."

"Maybe they did. But they're openin' again now. Look." Maury walked a few steps off the hummock and pointed. "See? One a the horses is liable to get a leg in there, an' break it." Then, "No, before we begin, I'll drop a scraperful a dirt in some of the bigger ones."

The fissures closed, they began the job. Maury managed the scraper. Pa Thor drove the horses. Kirsten put down a matting of willow twigs ahead of their work.

All morning the wind lifted, slowly, sniping at the tops of the dust dunes and the hard knolls and the bare willow trees and the single tall cottonwood. The sun baked the land, opening the fissures a little.

They worked steadily, wordlessly.

In the fields, the grain leaves curled slightly, and in the pasture, the grass became limp and pale.

That first noon, at twelve, the men laid off work for an hour. After stalling and feeding the horses, they went to the house. There they found that Ma Thor had poured out wash water for them in the shade along the north side of the shack. Pa Thor gestured for Maury to wash first. Kirsten went into the house.

Maury cooled his face in the water. He slapped soapsuds over his eyebrows and cheeks and into his ears. He dug for dirt on his face. He snorted and blew through the soap bubbles. It was pleasant to him. He remembered the good old days when he and Pa Grant had come up from the fields at noon, weary, hungry, yet full of pride in good work done on the land. He snorted, and rubbed his face. Hard work in the soil cleaned a man.

Behind him, Pa Thor coughed. He rubbed his leg with his dry, harsh palm. "By gosh, son, that was workin', huh?"

"Sure was," said Maury resoaping his arms.

"When two fellers set their mind to it, they sure kin do a lot a work in a day."

Maury nodded. He wished the old man wouldn't talk.

"Hell, if I'd had a man early this spring, this farm would a been right shipshape by this time."

"Huh."

"We'd a been ready to set sail across the prairie. If I'd a had a man." Pa Thor sighed.

Maury shrugged. He picked up the towel and began to dry his face.

"Well, we still kin do a hell of a lot together."

Maury gritted his teeth. If only the old man wouldn't talk about it!

Pa Thor rubbed his leg. "By God, this leg a mine. Sure is funny. Can't tell if it's just achin' a tiredness, or achin' from the rain that's comin'."

Maury shook himself, and before he could hold his tongue, said curtly, "Hell, it's achin' from tiredness. Just plain tiredness." Then, softening, he added, "At least, I know I'm plumb wore out."

Pa Thor said hastily, "Well, we'll take a little nap after dinner, son. Horses need a rest too. They was gant an' puffin' this mornin'. Sure, a man gets a little sleepy towards noon. It won't hurt none to get rid a that last little shake a sleep."

Maury said nothing. He finished drying his face. He felt sorry that he had shut up the old man so abruptly, but he resented having him intrude his rambling talk into the first good mood he had had in years.

IV

No CLOUDS CAME THE NEXT FEW DAYS. Mornings, the sky was as clear as a freshly washed window. And the crow of the roosters tinkered the silence with echoes. And white hens scurried like rolling cottonballs over the graying fields.

By noon of the third day, the wind rose and the skies began to fill with dust clouds. Yellow tints appeared in the grainfield and the inch-high corn hesitated in its precise rows.

Maury found the work on the dam brutal. Years of drouth had hardened the soil of the hummocks. The jerk and the rip and the draw of power in the handles of the scraper almost tore out the muscles of his back and arms. He discovered muscles he never knew he had. Sometimes, when he stood up to look over the land, the glimmer of the heat evaporating along the horizon and the whiteness of the gray soil beneath the staring sun made him dizzy. He longed for a few moments of rest. Sleep became a great goal in life.

Work brought out many memories he wanted to forget. While he kept his eyes on the dust and clods before the leaping scraper, and puffed on the cigarette burning beneath his nose, he recalled the days when he had worked his father's farm in Oklahoma, now gone up in dust. He remembered the old smell of horse sweat, the odor of his own sweat, the tug of the wet shirt on his working muscles. He recalled his mother's lined, hollowed face and his father's hopelessly gesturing hands. He recalled that four years ago he had sworn to himself with great solemnity that he would never again work on a farm, even if it were to be set down in the Garden of Eden.

Sometimes, when he stopped to think about it, he could not understand himself. How could he have taken up with these Thors? It was simple to see that their battling against this dust on the pale, shimmering prairie was utterly foolish. And yet, here he was, actually helping them. He shook his head.

Before he went to sleep at night, he found himself desiring Kirsten. The first day he had caught a pleasant whiff of sweat smells from her body, and, when she had bent over, glimpsed beads of sweat on the rise of her breasts. He had hungered to touch them.

Already, on the third day, beneath their feet, water licked at the barrier. The narrow opening that had yet to be filled became too small for the stream. Every day the backed-up water became deeper.

They had just dumped a scraperful of earth. Pa was driving the horses, Kirsten was weaving a mat of twigs ahead of their work, and Maury was guiding the handles of the scraper.

Maury said, "You know, Pa, I've been noticin' that by the time we get back here with a scraperful, the water's washed out the one before."

Kirsten looked up. "I was just gonna say the same thing myself."

Maury directed a squint at her, then looked back at Pa Thor. "Tell you what," he began, wiping the sweat off the end of his nose, "tell you what. If we was to have a couple a shovels handy right there on the bank, an' have 'em set up ready for grabbin', we could heave in enough dirt to plug that hole all at once."

"That's it!" said Pa Thor. "That's it." He paused to feel his back.

"Well, we'll do it right after we take a little rest, then."

Pa Thor sat down.

Kirsten stood near, seemingly tireless.

Maury seated himself on the upturned scraper. As he sat puffing, he rolled and lighted a cigarette.

Water murmured lightly beneath him. There was a little wind up, and dust drifted around their feet. The leafless willows sighed behind them. A solitary cotton-wood, a few of its lower branches glittering with yellow leaves, spread its webby shadow over the foot of the dam.

Maury kicked at a nearby clod of the scrambled earth. It opened up like a cracked egg, spilling black and blue-gray soil, and flakes of strange matter. Maury leaned forward to look at a piece of it. "Huh," he grunted. "Funny stuff. Looks like there was a lake here once. Clam shells, little ones. And fishbones." He picked up another piece containing a small, minutely-chambered nautilus. "Sure, there must a been water up here." Then, "An' here's an old fish skeleton."

Pa Thor came over to look. "Sure. An' there's . . . that looks like the print of a fern. Like Ma Thor had once. Sure."

Maury looked at a few more pieces. "Funny land."

"Well, it's like I said. A land full a history." Pa Thor paused, and stared at the dirt. Then he, too, picked up a huge clod and began to break it carefully apart. "Who knows, maybe we'll come across a dinosaur of our own."

"Fat chance," Maury grunted, swiping at the midge-flies buzzing near.

"Never kin tell, though, son. Never kin tell. We're close enough to the Bad Lands to have one pop up here."

"Aw . . ." Maury shook his head. "You're too full a dreams, Pa." He scratched his leg. "You know, by golly,

58

my leg hurts a little. A man'd think I was gettin' milk leg." Then, seizing on the idea, Maury asked, "Bet quite a lot a people hereabouts had milk leg, didn't they?"

"No. No. Never heard a one."

Maury laughed, looking at the old man slyly. "Aw, you can't tell me. Milk leg was everywhere where there was dust storms. Everywhere."

"No, not here. Was it, Kirsten?"

"No," she said, looking directly at Maury.

Maury shrugged. "I suppose the next thing you'll try to tell me is that it don't get cold here in the winter?"

"Well, now, that depends. I've gone to bed with it twenty below and woke up with it meltin' the snow on the roof."

"Huh!"

"Sure. That's right. When the chinook comes over the rockies, everything melts."

"Yeh. One a the few good winds there is, I suppose," Maury grunted, puffing on his cigarette.

Pa Thor rubbed his leg. He raised his pale eyes to look at the western horizon. He glanced at the yellow-green grain south of the dam. "Well, anyway, son, the grain's still pretty good."

"Huh. It ain't gettin' any greener."

"Well, it ain't gettin' any yellerer either. All it needs is a sprinkle a rain."

"Aw, hell, Pa. You . . ." Then, "Pa, I . . . Pa, I'll tell you one thing, I'm damned glad there's only an hour's work left on this dam."

"Son, I . . ."

"Damned glad. Because now I kin get a move on. Vamoose."

"But, look, son. The corn does look better."

"Christ, Pa, you must be blind. It looks even worse than the grain."

"Oh, but the corn will be all right. It always looks that way when it starts up. All it's doin' is settin' down its roots. Gettin' them anchored down deep so's it kin catch all the rain it kin when the rain comes."

Maury stood up. He tossed away his cigarette butt. He made a move as if to get the shovels.

"No, no, son. I'll get 'em. You set down. All I been doin' all day is drivin' the horses while you've been doin' the real work."

Maury sat down again.

And then Pa Thor sat down too. He worried a clod of dust. He coughed, and kicked at the ground. Presently he asked, "Well, it's final, then, you're goin'?"

"Yep."

"I sure could use a man this summer." He paused. "What's there on the road fer you?"

"Nothin'. It's just that I can't stand dyin' on a dust farm again."

"Son, tell me, where you gonna end up?"

"Oh, somewhere." Maury leaned over to pick up another clod of dried earth. "You see, Pa, I know it ain't heaven on the road. But look here. Suppose I was to get me a job that'd pay me three, four, five dollars a day. Say three. Three times five is fifteen. Suppose I get a cheap place to bunk. A dollar er so a week. An' I take it easy on grub, or cook myself. Why, I kin earn 'bout ten clear a week. Forty a month. In a couple a months . . . why, hell, man, I'll have enough to look around, maybe start a hamburger joint, somethin' I can run by myself. An' then I kin thumb my nose at the world. Tell it to get the hell out, or stay, just as I please. Think of it!"

Pa Thor scratched his gray stubbled chin. "Where'll you get a job like that?"

"I thought maybe . . . the Hills . . . the gold mines there . . ."

60

"An' if you don't?"

Maury looked at his shoe and then picked up another clod of dirt in his hand and broke it into powder. "Well, then, it'll be hell. Terrible. Because, you see, nothin' ever grows in the heart of a bum. Nothin'."

"Son. Son. There you go. There you go," Pa Thor said softly, his eyes almost closing.

"But I hate the dust bowl more, Pa."

Pa Thor's face fell. "So, then you are gonna leave us?"

Maury nodded.

Pa Thor stood up. "Couldn't you wait one more day?"

"Everything'll be all right with you an' Kirsten," Maury said, "without me."

"Naw. No it won't."

"Sure," said Maury, "sure." He looked at the dam. "Who knows? Maybe you got somethin' big here." He felt sorry for Pa Thor, so he added, as if in reverie, "Say, maybe you have at that."

Pa Thor slapped his leg. "By golly, now you're talkin'! You know, the grain an' corn still look good. I got a half a notion to ask the bank fer some credit an' buy a couple extry horses."

"Ain't Becky and Beaut enough?"

"Naw. 'Course, they's great horses. When it comes to real git an' pull, they kin work rings around any team a horses in this here county, comin' er goin'. But I need two more. I got two cultivators there, rustin' in the barn, an' I thought maybe me an' you could get at the corn together."

Maury rubbed his lips. He tried to act as though he hadn't seen a pathetic questioning in the old man's eyes. He shook his head faintly.

"Well," said Pa Thor, sagging a little, "well, maybe I'm dreamin'." He paused. "Shucks. Well, it's no use. Because even if I was to ask that banker down at Sweet

Grass, he wouldn't loan me his pen to sign my own mortgage."

Maury grunted. He had the feeling that Pa Thor had also aimed the remark at him.

Then Pa Thor, shrugging, left to get the shovels. He groaned a little as he walked away. And his left toe dragged a faint trace in the dust just after the imprint of the shoe.

Alone now, Maury sat across from where Kirsten stood. He shifted uncomfortably. He rolled another cigarette and lighted it nervously with the old butt. Then he tossed the butt into the water. He tried to think of something casual to say. Nodding toward the horses, he said, "They're puffin' a little."

Kirsten kept still. She sat down then and looked across the land.

"Yer ol' man's got a lot a hope," Maury said, watching Pa Thor hump steadily out of sight over the knoll.

Kirsten sighed, and then unbent herself. "Yeh, poor man. But you should have seen him last fall."

"Was it bad?"

She nodded briefly.

Maury considered his nicotine-stained fingertips and then looked directly at her, pulling up the wrinkles around his eyes tightly. "Tell me."

"Well, he just sat looking out of the winder all the time."

"That all?"

"All? Why! he set there for two whole weeks! Ma nearly went crazy. She rolled all up into a ball a nerves. An' she started to shake him. An' rattle him. An' slap him. Then, finally, when he still didn't say anythin', or do anythin', why! she turned sudden quiet, and her teeth showed. An' she asked, 'Pa, what's that winder-lookin' got that I ain't got fer you?'"

"What'd Pa do?"

"Pa got scared an' hoisted himself quick outdoors an' acted busy fer a day."

"Then what?"

Kirsten sighed. "Next day, he was lookin' out a the winder again, just lookin'."

Maury suddenly ached inside. He stood up and looked to see if any one were in sight. He rubbed sweat off his brow. He looked at her brown arms. He went near her. And even as he thought of reaching to touch her, there on the neck beneath the broad brim of her red-painted straw hat, she looked up at him. He bent down. His mouth fitted on hers hungrily, roughly.

She broke away from him instantly. "Gettin' crazy notions again, mister?"

Maury stood apart from her. "Kirsten, I . . ." He studied her. He would have sworn that he had felt her giving a little; but yet, there she sat, calmly straightening her clothes. He was puzzled, then exasperated; he had almost forgotten that he had intended to stay with them only one more day. Kirsten, and Pa Thor's hope, had worked on him.

"Rested?" Pa Thor called, as he came over the knoll, carrying shovels.

Maury nodded. He looked quickly at Pa Thor to see if he had seen them.

Pa Thor was nearly out of breath as he came up the top of the dam. He threw the shovels on the other bank. Apparently he had not seen.

Maury took a deep breath. He glanced briefly at Kirsten and then studied the shovels. There was something he had thought of doing. "Oh, yeah. Say, we'll have to loosen up some of that ground there afore we start scoopin'."

Pa Thor said, "You know, Kirsten, sometimes I think this feller here ain't as dumb as he looks."

Irritated by the remark, Maury attacked the bank of ground with a furious, stabbing shovel. He was in a hurry to finish the job and move on.

"Ain't that about enough?" Pa Thor asked presently.

Maury nodded. He threw the scoop aside and, picking up the lines again, drove the horses around and guided them across the dam to the stripping ground. He turned them again, facing them toward the dam and then set the scraper at a tilt, with the knife-edge into the earth a little. He waited for Pa. He saw Kirsten gathering branches in her arms again.

"Set, Pa? This'll have to be quick!"

Pa Thor took the lines from him. "Sure, let her rip!" He slapped Becky and Beaut and they leaned into their traces.

The scraper buckled beneath Maury. He held hard. He felt the knife-edge stub on a stone and, for a moment, feared he would be hurtled over the horses.

"Whoa!" Pa Thor shouted. "Whoa, there! Say, son, you'd better get another start, huh?"

Maury nodded. "I'll get it this time," he muttered.

The next time the knife-edge missed the stones.

"Better trot the horses, Pa, an' then swing 'em off to the left, quick. I'll dump her an' then grab the shovels."

Pa Thor hurried the horses. Their hooves pounded with a hollow sound on the narrow, unsettled ledge of the dam.

Maury ran behind them and the bumping scraper. He bent low, his hand on the handle of the scraper, ready to trip it.

Pa Thor swung the horses off to the left. "Okay," he yelled.

Maury heaved, and, with the same motion, leaped over

the gap and grabbed his shovels.

Kirsten was there before him and her shovelful landed in the gap ahead of his.

Pa was there an instant later. They worked steadily for some minutes without looking up.

Then Maury chanced a quick look. "We're gainin'!" he shouted.

They shoveled hurriedly.

As he worked, Maury was amazed to see Kirsten throw in as many heaps of dirt as he. He doubled his efforts.

"There," Pa Thor said at last, resting on his shovel.

Maury stopped. Puffing and sweating profusely, he watched the water rising against the dam. "I dunno. Maybe we'd better throw on a couple more there." He threw in a few more for good measure and then stamped down the soft earth. He kicked at a few clods, accidentally spilling a little dust in his pantleg cuff and into his shoe. He lifted his foot and dug at the dirt in his shoe and then kicked his foot out. He studied the dam.

Pa Thor had come up beside him. "Well, what do you think of her?"

"Okay." Maury nodded. "It's okay."

"It's a humdinger! Well . . . let's go eat. I'm hungrier than a bridegroom the mornin' after." Pa Thor forced a chuckle, and then added wryly, "I hope Ma's surprised us with some tapioca an' coffee."

V

WHEN MA THOR SET OUT a dinner of potatoes, flour gravy, and the Thor's last can of peaches, Maury choked on the food. He belonged here. He shook his head. He hated the long hours of waiting for freight trains on the wind-cut prairie, the blistering sun beating down on a glinting gravel road, the hunger of his wriggling stomach. He swallowed a glass of water and steadily kept his eyes away from the Thor family.

They finished eating. The men pushed back their chairs. Pa Thor lighted his corncob pipe, Maury his neatly-rolled cigarette.

The women still sat close to the table, looking with some pride at the empty plates, tasting the left-overs.

Maury stared out of the window.

Pa Thor coughed, and then said, "Well, Ma, get out the purse and pay the boy. He earned it, right square."

Ma Thor waited a moment.

"Go on, Ma. Get up an' get the boy his dollar. Go on."

Ma Thor stood up and went into the back room and after a moment came out with an old, scabbed leather purse. It was flat and deep, and almost empty. She reached in her hand, bowing her head a little as she stood near him, staring into the mysteries of the purse. A patient, melancholy expression worked on her face. Finally she drew out a few bills, picked them over, and drew forth a worn dollar bill. She looked at it a moment, rubbed it, and then handed it to Pa Thor.

Pa Thor took it, and then, with dignity, handed it to Maury. "That enough, son?"

"Hell, yes! Too much."

"No. No, it's not. If times were good, you'd get more."
He smoked thoughtfully on his pipe. "But you're satisfied? You won't be callin' us cheapskates when you're off
our yard?"

Maury mumbled, "No, 'course not!" and pocketed the
bill.

Pa Thor puffed a moment and then said, "Well, I'm
gonna take my catnap now, while the horses is restin'.
You nappin', too, son, before you go?" He rubbed his
leg slowly.

"Well . . . I dunno . . ."

"C'mon. You ain't in no hurry. Might as well."

Ma Thor said, "Sure. Take a rest afore you start
travelin' again, son."

"No. I'm anxious to be off. Thanks."

When Maury did not move right away, however, Pa
Thor settled back into his chair. He puffed nervously on
his pipe. Maury could feel the old man's eyes boring
into the side of his face.

Presently Kirsten got up and moved around a little,
gathering up the dishes.

"Well, I'll take a catnap," Pa Thor murmured again.
"An' then I'll drag out the cultivator an' start off the
year's corn."

When Pa Thor still did not get up, Ma Thor turned
on him and exclaimed, "Well, git to your bed, then,
man! Don't sit here complainin'. Git!"

Startled, slowly gathering his wits together, Pa Thor
stood up and shuffled off to the back room.

Maury was sorry he had not followed him. For now
he suddenly felt a great need for sleep. He wrestled with
the impulse for a while and then succumbed to it. He,
too, went to the back room and lay down on Kirsten's
bed. Her pillowcase had the clean smell of well-sudded
laundry.

When Maury woke, Pa Thor had gone. Maury jumped up quickly, rubbed his eyes and combed his hair with his fingers. He entered the kitchen where Ma Thor was sitting. The table was clean and the dishes were washed.

"Pa go?"

"Yes. He's out in the field."

"Kirsten?"

"I don't know. She's somewhere about."

He yawned. "Well, I guess I better go."

Ma Thor turned her chair and studied him with kind eyes. Her big red hands fumbled in her lap. Apparently she had been waiting for him to wake up. She brushed back her hair with the back of her sunburnt arm. "You're really goin'?"

"Yes, Ma. I just gotta." He pulled out a pouch of tobacco nervously, tightened his lips when the thin paper momentarily refused to fold in his fingers, poured out the tobacco, and then, gently rolling the tobacco back and forth, licked the paper's edge with his tongue. He dug into his pocket for a match.

"You're really a-goin'?"

"Why, dammit, yes," he exclaimed, now irritated.

Ma Thor sighed. Then she went into the back room and in a moment came out with something in her arms.

Maury recognized it instantly. She had neatly washed and ironed his spare shirts, and his spare overall had been washed and folded, too. He swallowed quickly. He growled at her affectionately, "Say, you shouldn't a done all that! Besides, who said you could go nosin' through my stuff?"

Ma Thor said nothing.

Maury packed the cleaned clothes into his bundle and then, hitching them up in his arms, said, looking off to one side, "Well, Ma Thor, I . . . well, so long. Thanks for the good grub."

"Ain't you sayin' good-bye to Pa?"

"Why, he ain't aroun' an' I . . ."

"Kirsten?"

"Well . . ." he laughed. "I don't think she'd care if I didn't."

"But Pa . . . he'll feel mighty bad if you didn't . . . bein' as you resemble Tollef so much."

"Aw . . ."

"Go out to the field and say good-bye to him."

Maury mumbled to himself, and then set down the bundles and went out the door and across the yard. He neared the barn before he saw Pa Thor across the prairie away, slowly driving Beaut and Becky across a cornfield that had just begun to check into rows of well-planted corn. Swinging his long legs over the barbed-wire fence, Maury strode toward the field.

Pa Thor had reached the end of a row as Maury came up.

"I came to say good-bye, Pa. Sure want to thank you fer bein' so hospitable to a stranger. Mighty nice a y'u."

Pa Thor got off the cultivator and strode around a little, holding his leg and then fumbling for his pipe. "Ain't nothin'. Do it fer most. What do you think a this corn, son?"

Maury looked down a long row. "It's good, it is."

"Sure is."

Maury's face wrinkled. He remembered the fields in Oklahoma with their green shoots. He had an impulse to get on the cultivator to plow one round before he left, just to get the old feel of it again, the thrill of holding the shovels close enough to the corn to stir up the dirt and kill the weeds, and yet not so close as to bury them under the splashes of earth. "Say, Pa, mind if I take it around the field once? I'd . . . kin I?"

Pa Thor quickly hid his eyes and looked into the

69

bowl of his pipe, narrowing and crossing his eyes to do so. "Sure. Go ahead. I'm stiff from sittin'. I'll walk along behind y'u."

Maury took up the lines and clambered aboard the out-thrust cultivator seat. He fitted the knotted lines over one shoulder and around his neck. He jiggled himself in the seat a moment and then, looking over the land briefly, snapped, "Giddap, boys. Git. Go."

The horses pulled into their traces and started up slowly. For a few moments Maury had difficulty with the shovels. The machine was an old one and dug either too deep or too shallow. He covered a few hills of corn. He heard Pa Thor running behind to uncover them. In a few minutes, however, he had the cultivator working smoothly.

Pa Thor looked searchingly over the prairie.

Maury, too, glanced up now and then from his work. He sensed Pa Thor's mood. "Pa, look at them hundreds a acres out there. It's nothin' but sand dunes. Miles of 'em."

Pa Thor was silent for a moment. He stumbled along, stretching his stiff legs. He coughed a few times and then relighted his pipe. "You know, son, you're right. Too right. You see the dunes an' the waste, and I can't deny that you see 'em. But you don't know some things. We send up a state senator from here an' he . . ."

Maury interrupted, "Huh! I'll bet it don't take him long to make the rounds a his constityunts!"

Pa Thor went on. Maury had slowed the horses a little and Pa Thor walked along easier now. "This state senator had a dream. He told us about it. He said if we was to put a new roadbed under the Highway it'd pull the traffic north off U.S. 20 an' maybe even off U.S. 30. An' tourists'd come through here thicker'n hoppers after a good crop. They'd be headed west fer the sights, see. An'

70

they'd spend money, lots of it, see. And the money would trickle down into the towns, an' then, pretty soon, trickle into the country. An' the country'd be a little better off."

Maury snorted. "What's that got to do with dirt farm-in'? Hell, Pa Thor, you're blind. That theory is wild. If anything, you ought to find some way of makin' them tourists stick here, break down their cars, so they'd hafta spend money. By buildin' 'em new roads they just fly through faster. Why, right now they fly so fast they don't even see this turribleness here!"

"Well, anyway," said Pa Thor, working his old teeth on his pipestem, "well, an' then this state senator said he was goin' to suggest to the legislature that they raise the tax on the feller that owns the gold mines in the Hills."

"Say! Them's the ones I'm headed fer, ain't they?"

"Yeh, I guess so."

"Huh!" Maury snorted after a moment. "That's what the senator tells you. But when he gets down there, you know what he does. Big Guts takes him out to a couple a banquets, gives him some mighty polite and compli-mentin' talk, puts him up in a good room somewhere, grubs him, warms him up good with some hot li'l tooties, an' then the mighty state senator begins to feel a little debt. A little debt that's just a little bit bigger than the little debt he owes y'u fer your vote. Aw, Pa, you ain't that dumb you believe in him?" Maury squinted at him.

Pa grinned. He rubbed his leg.

"No," said Maury, "No, you might as well face it, Pa. Out here we ain't got a chance."

Pa Thor rubbed his leg as he ambled along. "Well, maybe. Anyway, my leg is sure achin' up fer somethin' or other."

Maury felt uncomfortable in the presence of such ir-repressible optimism. "Pa, you got to face it. You got to face facts." He remembered something and then chuckled. "Like that United States Senator from Minnesota who got up to speak afore a bunch a farmers. He got up on a manure spreader an' he starts off and says, 'Fellas, an' fella farmers. We got to look the truth straight in the face, gotta get down to brass tacks, gotta grab the bull by the tail and look him right in the eye!'"

Pa Thor grinned again. "Well, that's one place to look to see if things is workin'."

Maury shook his head. "No, I'm through with country work. Through. Out here, if the banks don't gobble you up, the grasshoppers or the dust storms get you. They skin the land and leave it stickin' bare ass up all prickled with stubble."

They had reached the end. While Maury turned the horses around and then drove them across the end to start a new strip of plowing, Pa Thor filled his pipe.

When they had started up again, Pa Thor said reflectively, "Son, that last talk a yours there, that sounded like the talk of a radical."

"But it's the truth!"

Pa Thor blinked and started on another tack. "You know, I was talkin' to a truck driver the other day about bums, about bindlestiffs. You know, fellers I see standin' there at the corner where I found you, wavin' an' tryin' to catch them a ride. Well, I asked this truck driver, 'Do you give them coyotes, them drifters, many rides?' An' he says, 'Hell, no! I ain't got no renderin'-plant truck yet. Besides, a man kin never tell when one a them bindlestiffs'll bat you over the bean.' Son, you see now, things like that don't make road travelin' a good thing. It's degradin'. Much better to stay put and stick it out. Good times'll come again. God can't forget us forever."

Maury felt the horses tiring and, to ease them up, pulled back on the lines. "Well, I don't agree with you.

72

Most truck drivers got a pretty good heart. Even some a them that's got the sign 'No Riders,' even they give a guy a ride. The companies don't like it, but the drivers are decent. A man don't feel mean acceptin' kindness like that."

Pa Thor shook his head. "Remember me tellin' you about Ol' Gust, the well driller? Well, sometimes when business is bad, he takes to truckin' cattle to Sioux Falls. When the Guv'ment was buying all them cattle, he was right busy. An' he told me once that he didn't know what was worse, takin' hundreds a skinny cattle east to Sioux Falls, or pickin' up hundreds a skinny people, wimmen, chillern, an' men, west through this country on their way to the Coast. He didn't know which was worse."

They went down through a little dip in the field. A few tumbleweeds had collected in the shallow bottom of it. "Look there," said Maury, "look. Them Russian this-tles. That's all that'll grow here, besides you people."

Pa stiffened a little.

Maury went on as he pushed down the cultivator shov-els. "Rode with a geologist once. Guess that's what you call one a them fellas that knows about the ground. Any-way, he tells me there's a county south a here that's the driest spot on earth. Ain't had rain there fer four years. Said he never saw the beat. Said he saw some petri-fied cowtracks there that was standin' four inches above the ground. Said it was a cow that'd walked there once, years and years ago, in the rain once, an' she'd pressed down the dirt, an' then it dried, an' the wind blew away all the dust around it, an' left the pressed-down ground standin' there. The hill looked like a sow's belly to the sun, with two little rows a tits goin' over it."

Pa Thor nodded.

"Pa, when's the last time you had hoppers come through here?"

73

"Five years ago. Cleaned us out then. We had a pretty good start with the crops that year, too. Wasn't too dry."

"Pa, if we get more rain, you'll get a flood a hoppers again. Mark my word."

Pa Thor became grave.

"Hoppers are terrible," observed Maury. "Terrible. I seen where they ate up a green-painted wagon. They hit fer the green, all of 'em. Hit fer it so fast, so hard, they et it up afore they knew they'd made a mistake."

Pa Thor nodded. He hobbled along slowly.

"Pa, how come you ain't been chased off this place yet?"

Pa Thor jerked up straight. "Me? Chased off? Who would try to do that?"

"I dunno. The Guv'ment. Back taxes."

"Well, the Guv'ment got plenty from me. They cleaned me out of a couple quarters a land already fer back taxes. But they're leavin' me this one, I guess. Feller jus' comes aroun' once a year, looks, an' nods his head. Guv'ment is sick a the land, too, I guess."

"Outside a that, your land clear?"

"Yes, sir, son."

"That's pretty good, that."

Just then the horse, Beaut, snorted and reared, and then both horses came to a stop.

Maury stood up on the plow. "Huh? What the hell?" Then, "Well, I'll be damned!" Ahead, the earth had opened into a fissure, too wide for the horses to cross.

Pa Thor came up then and looked.

Maury glanced at Pa Thor meaningfully and then, with the air of one who has won an argument, drove around the fissure and went on. He said nothing.

Pa Thor puffed nervously on his pipe and stumbled after.

A little later, Pa Thor suddenly exclaimed, "Why,

look! There's Ol' Gust drivin' on the yard now. Wonder what he wants." Pa Thor heaved a sigh of relief.

Maury looked up with interest. They had reached the end of the row. He turned the horses around to face the new row, got off and dusted his trousers, and then rolled a cigarette. He looked toward the yard, watching a fat man rolling toward them.

"That's the feller I was tellin' you that my wimmen don't like. An', maybe, with right good reason. He's a hard-drinkin' well-driller, sometimes a trucker. If there's a drop a water in the whole state a South Dakota, he'll smell it out with his divinin' rods, he hates it so. Yep, drills wells . . . an' wimmen. Got a surprisin' way with the wimmen."

Ol' Gust was almost upon them when Pa Thor exclaimed, "Ol' Gust! You ol' walkin' bottle you, what brings you out here?"

Ol' Gust's voice roared over the land. "Oh, I just happened to come along an' thought I'd stop to pass the time a day with them wimmen a yours." He wiped his hairy mouth. He looked at Maury. "Who's this? Where'd you get this bag a bones, Pa?"

"Oh, the wind brung him to my door. He's a friend of the fambly, though."

Maury reached out a hand and greeted, "Howdy, sir."

Ol' Gust shook hands, and then removed his shapeless straw hat. He scratched his thick, shrubby hair which came down over his forehead to within an inch of his bushy eyebrows. A mop of gray, inch-long whiskers almost hid a pair of lively, jet-black eyes. His nose was irregularly streaked with sharp red veins. Large, flat-lobed ears waggled as he talked. When he broke into vehement speech, his bright red tongue waggled in his bushy moustache like a red fox trapped in brush. And Ol' Gust was bowlegged. He had a hard, round belly that jutted from his frame like a pail from a milkrack. Ol' Gust looked like a fellow who had done a lot of day-passing in his time.

Ol' Gust said, winking at Pa, "Does this jack have any hifalutin scruples against a drop?"

"I dunno," Pa Thor said.

Ol' Gust felt of his belly and then reached into his pocket. "Snort a li'l snort, kid?"

Maury asked, "What is it?"

Ol' Gust blew heavily through his whiskers. "What is it! He's insultin', Pa. Insultin'! Askin' what kind a brand I carry. A good man never refuses a drink. Specially if it's the real McCoy."

Maury asked tersely, "Well, what the hell is it?"

Ol' Gust waved his hand and snorted, "What the hell is it?" He shook his head gravely. "This younger generation! By golly!" Then he looked at Maury again. "What the hell is it? This here is my own special mix. It's Ol' Gust's Whiskey. But, of course, if you want some rotgut, I got some a that, too."

Maury relaxed a bit. "No, no, I guess I better not. That's one thing I keep away from."

Ol' Gust patted him on the shoulder. "That's the stuff, boy. Wish to Christ I hadna started. But Ol' Pa Thor here got me goin'. Them wimmen a his . . . say, sure it ain't the wimmen that's keepin' you away?"

"No."

Ol' Gust nodded. "That's fine." He swayed a little. "Wimmen are no good, my boy. Stay away from 'em. Just like water, wimmen are overrated. Some fool men take to water. Some to wimmen. And some to both." He looked at Pa, then winked at Maury. "Yep. Yes, sir. Leave the wimmen alone, boy. I kin tell you that."

Maury felt an impulse to laugh. But he felt, too, how the two men were rapidly endearing the country to him.

He observed quietly, "Leave 'em alone, I suppose, fer you?"

Ol' Gust laughed. "You got it. You got it. Well, how about a slug?" He held out his bottle to Pa Thor.

Pa Thor looked furtively over the land toward the house and then said, "Sssst. Let's pretend we're lookin' at the harness on this side a the horses here." He led Ol' Gust around with him and then took a good long swallow. "Boy!" he exclaimed. "Boy! That sure hits the spot!" His eyes sparkled as he wiped his lips.

"You're quite a drinker," Maury observed, looking at Ol' Gust.

"Yes sir," Ol' Gust bawled. "Yes sir. I was the twelfth calf in the family an' by the time they got around to me, the old folks ran out a morals. An' so I took to drink."

Maury pointed to Ol' Gust's stomach. "They weren't stingy with that, either, were they?"

Ol' Gust stroked his stomach lovingly, and then bit lustily off a plug of chewing tobacco. "No, they weren't. No, that's one thing they did do, pass me an extry belly."

Maury fingered his cigarette, and again a nostalgia for the old farm gossip and banter rose in him, and he walked quickly over to Pa Thor and took his hand and said, "Well, Pa, much abliged for everything. I'm goin' now."

Pa Thor swallowed and his eyes opened and then saddened. " 'Bye, son. Take it easy."

" 'Bye, Pa Thor." He turned to Ol' Gust. "Glad to have met you, sir."

"Same, partner. Don't take any wooden nickels."

Then Maury strode toward the farmyard, cursing himself for allowing people to work on him to a point where he could almost forget his plan for life.

He had not said good-bye to Kirsten, and he had an impulse to avoid her. But when he recalled that she had

77

been somewhat cool toward him, he went in search of her. He would give her a parting shot, a sarcastic comment of some kind.

Where was she? Ma Thor had been vague about where Kirsten had gone after dinner. Abruptly, it occurred to him that their only sow had been heavy with pig and that perhaps Kirsten was out in the barn bedding her down. It would be just like that golden-skinned heifer to know about the sow's time. Just like her and still be the virgin she was. She always seemed to be running around the yard with the superior look of a secret knowledge. He turned his course a little and headed for the barn. He swung his legs over the barbed-wire fence and came up to the door on the cow-barn side.

And then he saw her. On her knees beside the sow, she was rubbing its bristly head and neck and back, brushing the birth-webs from the eyes of the new pigs, and guiding the helpless, worm-like creatures to the milk-running dugs.

His eyes opened, his nostrils twitched. The smell of birthing was suddenly oversharp. The straw gleamed. The light in the cobwebbed window became golden, the sun upon the land white-hot, the shadows north of the barn black.

He blinked his eyes, and suddenly in a flash, recalled another afternoon when, as a child of six, he had stumbled into a neighbor's forbidden bedroom and had witnessed the secret cult of child-bearing. The wise helper he had seen bending over the female in distress was his mother, just as now Kirsten was aiding another in her birth pains.

He felt ashamed that he had seen her here, ministering to the sow. It was a sight for only a reverent man to see, not for one who came with stinging words.

He went quickly away and across the yard and sat

down on the curb of the well and buried his head in his hands.

Later, when Kirsten came up from the barn to wash her hands under the pump, he was still sitting on the well curb, bowed, his head deep in his rough hands. He was irritated that she should have come. He had not fully made up his mind to go. He did not want the warmth of her sweet voice to be the last drop to fill the otherwise bitter cup. He did not look up as she worked the pump.

"What's wrong?" she asked. "Hurt yourself?"

"No."

He could feel her study him with troubled eyes. "Did you an' Pa fight?"

He shook his head vigorously. "Oh no. No."

"Something must be wrong," she said.

"It's nothin'," he said. "Nothin'. It's just that I keep on bein' a prize jackass."

"But why?"

"Nothin'. It's nothin' atall."

Just then Ma Thor came out of the house. She called, "You stayin' fer supper?"

He hesitated, wavered. He knew he should go on. And yet, a warm supper . . . Besides, it was already too late in the day to catch the night freight at Long Hope. "Yeh, I kin stay fer supper all right."

VI

THEY HAD GONE TO BED EARLY.

Near morning Maury was awakened by a drumming sound. He lay quietly for a few minutes, not knowing, at first, where he was. When it became clear to him, he looked up, to see Ma Thor's gray face sad in the lamplight as she worked on her darning.

"What time is it, Ma?"

"About four."

Maury raised himself to a sitting position. "What you doin' up so early?"

She nodded in the direction of the door. "Lissen."

He listened to the noise a moment. "Oh. The wind."

She didn't move for a moment. She stared at him. She said, "Yes, a big wind."

Maury listened for a time. There was dust on the sheets. His mouth and fingers felt gritty with fine sand. "How long's it been blowin' up, Ma?"

"A long time."

"Funny it started in the night."

"Yes."

"It usually starts about noon, when it starts. Funny." He shook his head. Something more than a big wind was up, he felt. He was wide awake now. "What you doin' up, Ma?"

"Waitin' fer Pa. He's gone to put the animals in the barn. An' get sacks ready to put dust mufflers on 'em."

Maury remembered. One night in Oklahoma when he and Pa had gone outdoors to mask the cows, the black wind had been so strong that it had extinguished the flame in a kitchen lamp his mother had been carrying.

And she had stumbled in the dark house and had broken her leg. When they had come back, they had found her, tumbled on the floor by the table. He ground his teeth now as he remembered that ancient anguish. And, suddenly stubborn again, he growled, "Ma, wake me when it's five. I gotta get started today."

"I will, son."

Maury turned his back to her and lay like a stone.

The wind tore at the shingled roof and sprayed sand over his face. The house shook when the wind bore directly down upon it. Sometimes there was a steady banging sound, as if a door were slapping somewhere in the wind. The sound of the creaking gate outside was like the scratch of a spoon on a pan.

He snuggled deeper beneath his blankets. And, pressing his knees against his chest and his heels against his bottom, he dropped off to sleep again. He dreamed of Kirsten. He dreamed of hunger in a black, dry land.

When Ma Thor called him at five o'clock, Maury got up heavily. He spat dust out of his mouth.

Ma Thor set out a basin of water for him on the kitchen table, and beside it she laid out a plate and a fork and a knife and a spoon. Then she set out a cup of steaming coffee.

Just as he finished washing, Kirsten stumbled out of the back room, her hair straggling over her cheeks, her eyes thick with sleep.

Maury, excited, and full of tolerance now that he was going on, stooped to a little flattery, and said, "Well, here's one woman who looks pretty in the mornin'."

Ma Thor smiled briefly and rubbed her hand over Kirsten's brow. "Yes, Kirsten is a good girl."

Kirsten murmured something unintelligible.

Ma Thor said, "Now, now. You better go wash your face. It'll make you feel better." She pushed Kirsten

81

toward the sink and then went to the stove for the cooker of tapioca and poured some out in Maury's plate on the table.

As he ate the hot gruel, he watched Kirsten bending over the sink. Her dress lifted a little. He saw the soft flesh of her thigh. Catching himself scheming again, he looked quickly down at his plate.

For the first time, he noticed that the food was gritty with fine sand. He shivered each time his teeth bit on a grain of it.

By the time he had finished his breakfast and lighted a cigarette, Kirsten had finished her washing and had combed her hair. She looked bright again. He watched her peering through the window to the east, where it had begun to lighten.

Kirsten turned. "You're goin'?"

Maury nodded.

She hesitated, looked once more at him, and then quietly went over and began to roll up his bundles for him.

He watched her a moment, startled by the meaning of her gesture. Abruptly, he jammed his cigarette into his plate and went over and pushed her away to pack the bundles himself.

Finished, he turned, looking off to one side toward the floor. "Well, so long. I'm gonna try it." He glanced briefly at Ma Thor, then at Kirsten, and, turning, quickly picked up his bundles and stepped outdoors into the black wind. He was glad that Pa Thor had not been in the kitchen. He would have found it hard to bid the old man good-bye.

After a struggle, he came upon the edge of the gully and dropped quickly into it. But the ditch beside the road gave him little protection. The dust fell thickly on him, filling his mouth and his eyes. He spat fiercely and blinked as he fought his way to the corner.

He stood there a little while. It became light enough to see objects vaguely. He looked up the road and waited. There was a real dust storm roaring in, all right. He could not see more than twenty feet in any direction. His clothes became heavy and clogged with the dust and sand. He worried about his guitar, that it would fill with dust and lose its tone.

His lips drew back into a bitter, wrinkling grin. He blew his nose. He coughed and spat with the wind. He cleared his throat. He could feel his lungs become sore. He leaned into the wind. But no car came.

He endured it for an hour before giving up.

And when, finally, he did turn to go back to the Thors, he felt broken inside. He went to the door despondently. Without knocking, he opened it and entered.

Kirsten jumped up from her chair. He saw her repress a quick smile.

Ma Thor calmly walked to the stove and picked up the coffee pot. She refilled his cup.

The hours went by slowly.

Maury sat in Pa Thor's chair by the window. He felt guilty about not going to help the old man, who was still in the barn, but he could not find it in himself to fight the storm.

It was Kirsten who went out to help.

The hours lifted the morning into noon. The wind continued to raise the surface of the earth into the sky. The grass in the pasture and the hay land, and the young corn, lay bent against the ground. They became brown and riddled, and black-edged holes opened in the stems and the leaves.

They were in the house. Pa Thor had come in again.

He sat in his armchair near the window, looking dolefully out into the bruising storm. Kirsten worked over a dress. Now and then she stood up, put her hand on Pa Thor's shoulder and looked with him into the darkness outside. Maury tried to read an old magazine by the light of the fluttering kerosene lamp on the table. Ma Thor patched on a pair of overalls.

Once, Maury, watching the wind shake out its long black arm at him from the south, tried to ease the feeling in the room. "You know, Pa, the way the wind's been blowin' from the south, I expect any day now to see my Pa's Oklahoma farm come flyin' by on its way to North Dakota."

But no one said anything. No one shrugged in answer.

Quite without warning, Ma Thor began to make a weird sound, like a whistle rattling before it breaks into a scream.

Maury jumped up and stared at her.

Ma Thor was staring out of the window, her eyes opened very wide, her nostrils flaring, and her face very white except for a red patch over her right eye which seemed to throb like a heartbeat.

For a second, Maury had the fleeting impression that Ma Thor was acting a little. Her actions, coming on so suddenly, seemed to have an unreal quality about them. But it was her voice that convinced him that there was something really wrong.

Pa Thor had jumped up too, as had Kirsten. Pa Thor leaned over her. "What ails y'u, woman?"

She continued her strange gurgling, her staring. Her face began to work a little.

Maury was sure she was having an epileptic fit. He had once seen a hoboing buddy of his have one.

Pa Thor shook her. He was very frightened. "Hey, woman, cut it out! Are you goin' nuts, woman?" He shook her. "Come now. Use some sense!"

"Don't Pa," Kirsten was saying, "don't hurt her. You old fool."

"Damn it, I'm not hurtin' her. I'm only tryin' to find out what's the matter."

Then Maury understood. It wasn't epilepsy. He came around. He took Ma Thor's face in his big hands and looked into her eyes. Suddenly, he slapped her violently on the cheek. And, when she did not respond, he hit her again. A third time. Then she came up out of darkness. And her eyes rolled, and she sighed.

When her eyes had cleared, and she seemed to be with them again, Pa Thor sucked in a long nervous breath and then let it out with a great blast. "Httth! By God, woman, you had me goin' there fer a minute. What the hell was ailin' y'u?"

"Don't bawl her out, Pa," Kirsten begged.

"Bawl her out? Bawl her out? Who the hell wouldn't bawl out his wife if she started to act like a crazy one. Huh?"

"Well," she growled, "well . . . she didn't mean to do it."

Pa Thor snorted.

Maury was surprised by the old man's vigor. He hadn't expected him to react to danger as violently as he had. But he said nothing. It was their affair, not his. He went back to his chair, after making sure that Ma Thor had come back to her senses.

Pa Thor slowly went back to his chair, too, eyeing his wife with misgivings. As he settled down, he rubbed his leg slowly, muttering to himself.

Ma Thor sighed. She shook her head. "I sure felt funny," she murmured. "I sure felt funny. So funny." She looked at the floor. Her eyes seemed to be contemplating a great catastrophe. She had the vague eyes of a person

85

who has almost died through heart failure.

But Pa Thor was not satisfied. His existence had been shaken. He demanded an explanation for it. "What ails y'u, Ma? Tell us."

"I dunno. Dunno. I . . . it was so funny." Then, "Maybe I was worryin' too much. All this dust. It'd make anybody go crazy."

Pa Thor cleared his throat a little angrily and spat into the fuel box near the stove. "Take it easy, Ma. It ain't half as bad as you make it out to be. It'll be all right." Then a smile wrinkled the crow's-feet around his eyes into sharp lines. "My old leg's been achin' like blazes all morning. I ain't said nothin' because nobody believes me. But, really, it's never ached like this in a dust storm before. Somethin's up."

"Well, I hope so," Ma Thor whispered.

Pa Thor slapped his leg. "Sure, you just set down now an' quiet yourself." He rubbed his leg vigorously. "You know, this leg is really achin' now!"

Moved by the old man's affection and by his instinctively optimistic response to any danger, Maury observed then, "You know, my old blood-poison cut, down in my foot here, it's achin' up for the first time in years, too. Maybe there is somethin' in the air!"

"Sure," said Pa Thor. "Why sure. Just set tight here, everybody, an' it'll be all right." He filled and lighted his corncob pipe.

Maury felt a little torn inside. He hadn't believed all he had said, but he felt deep pity for Ma Thor. He talked on. "Why sure. This ain't bad. Wait'll it gets as bad as it did down in Oklahoma a couple a years ago. Why, shucks, one time the Big Wind kept blowin' night and day fer forty days, kept right on blowin'. Got so bad down there that there was about three foot of solid dust layin' all over the land. An' the people got pretty worried about that

time, an' they started to hold prayer meetin's. They invit-
ed over a lot of prayin' ministers, this one and that one,
tryin' 'em all out. But none of 'em worked. An' so then
one day, they heard of a rain-prayin', rain-makin' itinerunt preacher over in Missouri. An' they called him.
An' he came. An' he looked at the land, an' at the people, an' offered a prayer. An' he'd hardly started when
the raindrops began to fall. The itinerunt preacher
give one more blast a prayin', then blessed the people,
an' left fer home. Well," Maury paused for breath,
pleased that the gift of invention had not deserted him
in this moment, "well, it rained. It rained an' rained. It
rained so hard so long so fast, that the water stood all
over. An' the three foot a dust turned into three foot a
mud. An' everybody got stuck in it. The cattle an' horses,
everybody. An' so, finally, they had to send a delegation
to that preacher, to ask him to come back an' ask God
to call it off. An' the preacher came. An' he looked at the
swampy fields and the washed-out roads. And it looked
so hopeless, he said, 'God, I did ask fer rain, but, Christ,
this is ridiculous!' "

Pa Thor laughed and slapped his leg. He rolled in his
chair. His pipe almost fell from his mouth. "That's a
good one! A good one!" he roared. Then he narrowed
his eyes. "I can just see him standing there, I kin. Just
see him." He laughed again. "God, I did ask fer rain, but,
Christ, this is ridiculous!" He slapped and rubbed his
leg.

The womenfolk looked down, vainly trying to restrain
their smiles.

"Reminds me," ruminated Pa Thor aloud, as if he
hadn't noticed either Ma Thor or Kirsten. "Reminds
me. Neighbor Grayson down the road a piece, had a wife
ready to give with child. He was worried about her, worried more than most farmers are. Because, you see, she

was awful small. So he took her to Sioux Falls. That's where all them rich an' high monkey-monks live. An' while he was waitin' fer the kid to come, another feller came out, an' sat down to wait too. He was a fat rich feller, had all the sugar in the coffee he wanted. An' they set there waitin'. Pretty soon a nurse come out. 'Mr. Jones?' That was the rich feller, an' he sings out, 'Here. Yes?' 'Mr. Jones, you're the father of a nice, fat, eight-pound baby boy.' 'Great guns!' he roars. 'That's wonderful!' He jumps up and down, an' kisses the nurse and offers my neighbor a cigar. 'Here. Take two. Celebrate with me. It's wonderful, having babies! You're waiting too, I suppose?' My neighbor nods a little, nervous, you know. The rich feller says, 'Say, just to show you what kind of a good sport I am I'll wait an' keep you company till you hear from your wife.' So they set there, an' pretty soon the nurse comes out, an' she says, 'Mr. Grayson?' 'Yes.' The nurse was a little nervous an' she acted kinda funny, an' then she said, 'Well, you had a boy.' 'Oh,' he said. 'Oh. An' how much did it weigh?' The nurse wasn't gonna answer him at first, but finally she said, 'Well, it was about a pound.' Grayson thanked her an' started up to go out. 'Great guns!' yells the rich feller, 'only a pound? That's tough luck, feller. Tough!' 'Hell no,' says Grayson. 'That's not tough. Livin' out where I do, in the dust bowl, why hell! we're lucky to git our seed back.' "

Maury laughed, and, unconsciously imitating Pa Thor, slapped his leg too.

"That's enough," Ma Thor said sharply. "That's enough. No need to get funny. Stories is all right, but none a that kind. Pa, you've been around Ol' Gust too long fer your own good."

Pa Thor then played up a whine, cunningly. "Why, Ma, that story wasn't bad. I tol' you that one last year an' you laughed about it then."

"Oh, shut up," she said, getting up from her chair and hustling toward the pantry. "It ain't fittin' fer a person to hear such stories. Not at all. It's very degradin'. What kind a uplift is there in them fer the soul?"

Pa Thor laughed. "Why, Ma, I didn't know you was such a high class woman! Why, Ma!"

Ma Thor turned her face to hide a smile.

It was Kirsten who first noticed it. She jumped up, went to the window, and exclaimed, "Say, I believe it's quittin'. Sure. Look." She ran to the door and opened it.

And it had quieted. Sinisterly so. It was as if they had all been pulling mightily on a rope and now, as the rope gave away, felt themselves falling without support. They rubbed their ears and listened.

Then they all got up and went to the door to stand beside Kirsten. They looked over the land. They looked at the sky.

Maury pointed. "Look! Look up there. There's a hole in the sky . . . an' there's a cloud . . . a great one!"

Above them towered an immense thunderhead, creamy in its richness, and towering like a mountain peak. They could see the cloud moving in from the northwest. Great palisades of dust partly obscured the white, fluffy tops of the heaven-high cloud, and hid the dark blue bottom of its belly. The wind had been coming in from the south all day, but now, with the wind abating, an invisible wall moving ahead of the cloud pushed the dust back into the south. Lightning suddenly cut down through the middle of the cloud and speared the earth. Thunder blasted, rattled, and died away.

They stepped outdoors together and waited tensely beneath the war in the sky.

Then Maury pointed again. "See. Look! The two winds are comin' together. Look at them pieces a clouds

89

sluggin' around! Just like somebody's beatin' them with a big whip." As he yelled, he felt like a little boy at play again.

Small fragments of mist fluttered wildly in the opening between the dust cloud and the rain cloud.

"It's gonna rain at last," Pa Thor breathed. "I told you people my leg had a special ache today. By God, if there ain't a powerful rain storm brewin'!"

And even as he spoke, they heard a gradually increasing roar, its drone swollen with rumbles of thunder.

Maury shadowed his eyes with his right hand and looked along the horizon.

Just then the setting sun pierced the underside of the thunderhead with a long shaft of brilliant red light. There was a long dark column beside it.

"Tornado!" he whispered.

"No!" Ma Thor whispered.

"No!" exclaimed Kirsten.

"Aw, no. Not now," Pa Thor cried.

They stood stiffly, awestruck at the coming disaster.

Then Maury moved. "It's comin' all right. And right this way. C'mon. Where shall . . . down in the gully! Quick!"

But Kirsten broke away from them, running fleetly toward the barn.

"Where you goin'?" Maury shouted.

"The little pigs! The little pigs!"

"To hell with the little pigs!"

Kirsten shook her head and ran on.

Maury bounded after her. He caught her halfway across the yard. "You goddamn fool you. You goddamn fool. You're worth more than all the pigs in the world!" He grabbed her roughly, threw her over his shoulder like a sack, and ran back to the house with her. "Hurry," he shouted to Pa and Ma Thor. They still stood stupe fied, fascinated into immobility, staring at the snarling hose-like snake writhing toward them with an ever-increasing whining roar.

With his free hand, Maury grabbed Ma Thor's arm. Pa Thor shuffled after them, running backwards, facing the tornado. Maury pushed Kirsten down the bank of the gully. Ma and Pa Thor scrambled after her. Then he tumbled down, too. "Lay down as flat as you can! Flat!" he commanded.

Then the crazy, dancing, ripping roar of dust was on them.

Then, abruptly, there was a great quiet.

They sat huddled against the side of the gully's wall. They waited.

Presently, Maury crawled slowly up the side of the gully. He looked carefully to the northwest, to the southeast. He sighed. "Well, it missed us. And," he added casually, "if you'll stick out your hand, you'll find it's rainin'."

"By God, if it ain't!" Pa Thor exclaimed. "Christ! This ain't ridiculous atall!"

VII

AFTER A TAPIOCA SUPPER, they went out to sit on the stoop.

The ten-minute rain had cleared the sky of dust and sand. The sun was setting with a luminous red. Long shafts of purple and orange pierced the bowels of the re-treating clouds. Their creamy folds and rising towers of gold spread against the blue. A wind came softly from the west, carrying the scent of green corn and soaked grain. The ground itself had a new smell.

Kirsten, sitting beneath Maury on the lower step, her bare feet in the soft mud, her overall pantlegs rolled up, turned suddenly and said, "Maury, why don't you play us a little something on your guitar?"

"Naw."

"Please do. It . . . this is a sort of a holiday."

"No." He remembered he had once sworn not to, and he was stubborn enough to hang onto a foolish pledge.

Pa Thor nudged him then. "Go ahead, son. We ain't got no radio or no phonograph. We ain't heard music since goodness knows when. Go along now, an' get your guitar."

"But I ain't much of a player. I only play fer myself an' ain't much good."

"Well . . ." Pa Thor shrugged. "Well . . ."

Maury stood up suddenly. "Aw . . . All right."

And soon he began his tuning. They watched him intently, craving the sound of the twanging chord. He was embarrassed at first. He fingered the strings. He sought a haphazard tune in his memory. But it would not come. The only tune he could think of had a special meaning.

Presently he sang it—

> *I'm lookin' pretty seedy now while holdin' down my claim,*
> *An' my vittles are always too much the same.*
> *The mice play slyly 'round me as I nestle down to rest*
> *In my little old sod shanty in the west.*
>
> *The hinges are of leather and the windows got no glass,*
> *I hear the hungry coyote slink in the grass,*
> *The old board roof is warping, the blizzards try the frame*
> *Of my little old sod shanty on my claim.*
> *My claim . . .*

His strong chords drummed on the still, dusk air. A rapture lifted his face. And theirs.

> *Oh! bury me not on the lone prairie,*
> *Where the coyotes howl and the wind blows free.*
> *Blows free . . .*
>
> *Oh! bury me not on the lone prairie,*
> *Where the rattlers hiss and the grass runs free.*
> *Runs free . . .*

Ma Thor sat upright for a while. And then slowly she relaxed. Once, when Maury looked at her, he saw that her eyes had closed and that she was resting her head on Pa Thor's shoulder, and that Pa Thor's arm was firm around her. Immediately, the low chords deepened and the light chords became more tender.

And then Kirsten began to sing, softly at first, as if her voice were not sure of the tune—

> *I've reached the land of desert sweet*
> *Where nothing grows for man to eat.*
> *We have no wheat, we have no oats,*
> *We have no corn to feed our shoats.*
>
> *O Dakota land, sweet Dakota land,*
> *As on thy fiery soil I stand,*
> *I look across the plains*
> *And wonder why it never rains,*
> *Till Gabriel blows his trumpet sound*
> *And says the rain's just gone around.*

I've reached the land of hills and stones
Where all is strewn with buffalo bones.
O buffalo bones, bleached buffalo bones,
I hear your moans, I hear your groans.

Maury softened his strumming. He pulled the deep chords easily, lifting her voice sometimes, shading it again and then pulling it down. The lemon voice rolled around on the yard and echoed off the barn and ran over the prairie.

As suddenly as it had begun, the voice stopped. Maury's guitar went on alone, and then, hesitant, like a little boy without the hand of his elder sister, the guitar trembled. The notes fell from it like the sound of water dropping on dust.

Then, the mood changing, he sang, "Hallelujah, I'm a Bum," and in a moment Kirsten, laughing, joined him.

A long time later, they stopped, tired.

Pa Thor said, "That's fine good music, children."

"Play some more," Ma Thor whispered. "Play some."

"Yes," said Pa Thor, tightening his arm over Ma Thor, "yes. Play some more. Play that one about the 'dreary Black Hills'."

Maury looked at him quickly, wondering what the old man had in mind. He searched out the tune in his memory—

Kind friend, to conclude, my advice I'll unfold,
Don't go to the Black Hills to hunt for your gold;
The gamblers will fleece you of your new dollar bills
If you take the trip to those dreary Black Hills.
Black Hills . . .

Maury smiled a little, and then searched for other tunes. He became inventive. The fresh earth talked. He spilled fresh notes around, soft chords that rose and fell, that swelled and quivered like grass filling with rain and then bursting into seeds and then withering beneath the hot sun. He composed new words and new notes as he went along, told them about his aches as he waited along the corners of lonely roads, told them of watching the sky for clouds, told them of his hunger for thunder and lightning, told them of his fear of death, told them of his life in Oklahoma—

> Gone from the land, dead is my Pa.
> Gone from the shack, dead is my Ma.
> Gone from the plow, gone from the cart,
> Gone is this bum, dead is his heart.
> His heart . . .

Abruptly, tune and words became light-hearted—

> Oh! he was smiles and sweet wiles
> When they met by the fire.
> Oh! she was wise to the lies
> Of that dirty black liar.
> Liar!
>
> Oh, he was slick, he was quick
> When they set by the fire.
> Oh! she was turned, she was burned
> By that dirty black liar.
> Liar!

Then, suddenly, he stopped.

Kirsten turned. "Play some more," she whispered.

"No," said Maury. "No, no more. That's all."

Kirsten looked at him.

In the half-pink light, Maury was stirred by her face. "You look like you've been somewhere," he said.

"I have," she answered.

Maury looked down. He carefully covered the guitar and then shut the case.

"'S matter, son, tired?" Pa Thor asked.

"No."

"Play some more then."

"No. No more."

Ma Thor stirred. "It was nice. Real nice."

95

Maury set the case behind him and then leaned forward, resting his chin on his knee.

Pa Thor asked, "Why don't you play some more, son? We don't hear anythin' like that. Not out here."

Maury had been looking west toward the creek. "I wonder," he began, "I wonder . . . say, you know, we never thought a lookin' to see if that tornado ripped up our dam."

Pa Thor jerked upright, jolting Ma Thor and almost upsetting her. "I never thought of it either. We better look."

Kirsten jumped up too.

Maury looked at her. "Let's just you an' I go look," he said meaningfully.

A shrewd gleam appeared in her eyes. Then she nodded coolly. "All right."

They started together.

Pa Thor exclaimed. "Hey! What's the idea! I'm goin' too. Wait up."

Ma Thor came out of her dream. "Pa! Pa. Set here. You set here by me. Let the young ones go."

Pa Thor blinked, then understood. He relaxed a little, but not until he had rolled out a little growl to satisfy a sense of injured pride.

Maury and Kirsten went slowly across the yard, slipping in the mud.

Kirsten opened the gate near the barn and then closed it after them.

Maury pointed to her feet. "Your shoes?"

"What about 'em? I like to walk in the mud. Don't often get the chance."

"Say! I think you got something there. I ain't done it fer a long time either. Wait a spell." And he leaned over and unloosened his shoes and hung them on the fence near by. The mud was cool and soft to his feet.

They walked along together. There was only a faint glow in the west now. It was dark, and the stars were bright and sharp above them.

Maury looked up and smelled deeply. "You know," he observed, "that skyful of stars there now. It's just like a blue-black dress I've seen."

"Polka dots?"

"Yeh. Yeh. That's it. Polka dots." He took another deep breath. He looked down. He sloughed his feet through the mud. "Rain didn't go very deep. Just tied down the mud a little an' soaked the top."

"Won't this rain help none?"

"Depends on the kind a weather we get tomorrow. If it's hot, it won't do much good. Fry the stuff. If there's a mist, an' clouds, it'll do some good."

Kirsten remained silent.

He reached for her hand in the twilight.

She permitted him to hold it for a way and then released it.

Maury became uneasy. He tried to think of something to say.

Then they were near the dam.

"Tornado missed it all right," he said.

Kirsten nodded.

He looked at the narrow, shining fold of water. Star reflections were knitted together on the undulating surface. "Say!" he exclaimed. "Say, I'm gonna wash my feet." And he sat down on the edge of the dam and rolled up his pantlegs. He thrust his feet into the water. "Jeez!" he exploded, suddenly jerking them out again, "Jeez, it's cold!"

"Sure, you silly! Water's always cold after a rain."

Maury dropped his feet in again.

Kirsten looked at him a moment and then settled beside him. She pulled her overall pantlegs up high over her knees. Her flesh gleamed in the dusk.

Maury could dimly see her firm limbs, her arched back. He said, "I see you wear an overall right along."

"I don't like dresses. They clutter up so."

They splashed their feet in the water. He looked upward, watching a few streaks of clouds thicken and thin beneath the stars. As he fumbled for cigarette makings, he saw something move along the other bank. He studied it sharply for a moment and then laughed. "Danged tumbleweed had me scared fer a minute. Must be a li'l wind out."

Kirsten slapped water over her knee and then lifted a handful to her nose. "Smells good," she said.

But Maury had begun meditating. "You know," he said, "I'm not any smarter than that tumbleweed there. I'm driftin' back an' forth over the country, not getting any place. The wind blows west and I roll west. The wind blows east, and I roll east."

Kirsten said matter-of-factly, "Well, if it bothers you so much why don't you stay put here?"

"No," he said. "No, I couldn't do that. 'Course you got a little rain today, an' you got a dam started, but . . ."

Kirsten waited.

Maury said, puffing slowly on his cigarette and breaking a stick he had found into small bits with his fingers, "I remember one time when I was thumbing my way through Pennsylvania. The long hills there was like the shanks of a woman. They were good hills, they were. Soft hills. Not hard." Maury moved his feet slightly and slapped them in the water. He studied the eddies and then went on. "Well, I was tired one day an' I lay down in the grass, an' I saw a thin green worm crawlin' on the end of a blade of grass. I watched it, reachin' an' lookin' an' reachin' fer some place to go. It reached an' reached, an' finally . . . I pushed another blade a grass so the worm could reach it. Then it crawled down an' hid in the deep roots."

Kirsten rubbed her legs, looking at him wonderingly.

"Sometimes I gotta feelin' that you people are pushing a blade a grass fer me."

"Maybe we are," she said.

"I thought so."

"Anything wrong in that?"

Maury made a gesture toward her and then became deeply interested in his cigarette. He puffed at it a few times and then snapped it through the air. It made an arc of yellow fire and hissed as it hit the water.

"Naw," Maury said finally. "No. I couldn't do it. Couldn't live here. I can't fergit how my Pa an' Ma suffered. I don't wanna see it again. A man shouldn't have a brain, shouldn't have a memory." He rubbed his chin. "A memory is an awful thing," he said fiercely. "An awful thing. I once knew a guy down in Kansas. Swell fella, too. Met a gal. Married her and when the little kid came along, she died. He couldn't get no doctor. An' then the guy went on livin' on the ranch anyway, jus' tryin' to get on alone. But he couldn't fergit. Saw her dancin' in front of his eyes all the time. So he took to whiskey, an' then he croaked hisself one night."

Kirsten pulled her feet out of the water and rolled over on her stomach, holding her head in her cupped hands. She watched him.

Maury went on. "Yeh, knew another guy, too. Swell guy. Met him in a bindlestiff camp in Omaha. A fella could tell he had class. White hair. Back as straight as a broomstick. Full a guts. Nobody knew him well. Knew nothin' about him, 'cept that he had class. An' when he passed out, they found he was a big shot, a count from over in the Old Country. Sure he was. This guy came to America to fergit somethin'. Tried to make some money, too, to keep his title polished. Took his wife an' kid with him. Lost all his dough, an' then his wife and kid got some kind a sickness. I think it was milk fever. Then he couldn't get work. An' there he was, a count in a bum's stall. Kirsten, stuff like that is awful. Never will fergit him standin' one day on the edge of a hill. I came up to him and called out the time a day. But he didn't hear me. I called two or three times, but he didn't hear me. Finally, I poked him. Then he woke up. Shoulda seen his face. God, it was awful! The fella jus' couldn't fergit, is all."

Kirsten said slowly, "You've seen a lot of bad things, haven't you?"

Maury went on, deliberately trying to shock her. "Yeh. Well, yeh, guess I have. Never will forget that guy who had cancer in his backsides. Blllll! God, it was awful!" Maury shook his head involuntarily as the image came back to him. "When I asked him how he felt, he'd say, 'Okay, I'll be okay tomorrow.'"

"Didn't he know?"

Maury withered her with a sharp glance. "Why sure, he knew!" Maury pulled up his leg and ran his fingers between his toes. "Sure. He just had guts. An' I couldn't eat fer a week, an' everytime I pulled out my handkerchief, I could smell the guy."

Kirsten remembered a story now. "Our family's pretty tough, too. Take Uncle Holger once. He really looked like a kind man, all smiles, like he couldn't move a speck a dust fer fear he'd hurt it. An' yet, way inside, he was made a rock. We was there once fer Sunday dinner. An' he was prayin' along with a long prayer. All of a sudden he stopped. Everybody looked up, wonderin' what next. Uncle Holger jus' got up an' pulled out a tooth with a pair of pliers and then went right on prayin' an' thankin' God."

Maury said sarcastically, "Yeh, that's the one thing

your family ain't short on. Guts. Huh! Too much guts. Blind fool guts."

Kirsten was silent.

Maury looked at her and then rolled another cigarette. He heard the water slapping against the bank beneath them. "Look," he said, describing a semi-circle with his arm. "Jus' lissen now. What do you hear out there? Nothin'. Nothin'. Why! a man should be hearin' frogs croakin' after a good rain like that! There should be crickets. Peepers. Why! even them dumb bunny little cottontails, them dumb little bunnies has pulled out. Them little animals got more sense than you people have. They knew it was no use, an' gave up an' croaked."

Kirsten stiffened. She did not answer.

Maury puffed reflectively on his cigarette. He thought to himself for a time and then added, sadly, "A man hates to see his work go fer nothin'. A man hates to see his work go up in smoke. He hates to sin against his own soul." He paused and puffed on his cigarette again. He rubbed his hands together. The callouses in his hands squeaked.

Kirsten sat up. She said quietly, "Them's long words, mister."

Maury shrugged. He watched the rippling stars on the sleek surface of the water and then looked up at the sky. He straightened suddenly. "Hey! Look! There's a bat flyin' around!"

She followed his pointing finger.

He watched its irregular flight above them. He saw it disappear into the willows. Then he said, "Now, how do you suppose that bat makes a livin'?"

Kirsten looked down.

"Can't figger it out," he said, still musing. "It sure is funny. I ain't seen a bird fer so long I get all hepped up just seein' a bat." He puffed on his cigarette and then tossed it into the water. "It's just like when you're standin' along the road, waitin' fer a shiny new car and instead, a dirty cattle truck shows up. But you get all hepped up because you're sure you're gonna get a ride. Your heart pounds. Your fingers tingle. And then you wave. You actually smile. The fella comin' along is Christ comin'. He's gonna save you. Pick you up an' give you a chance."

"That's terrible!" exclaimed Kirsten suddenly. "Terrible!" Her voice was full of commiseration. "Terrible that a good man like you has to get thinkin' things like that!"

He studied her words in silence. He was pleased by the warmth in them.

They sat quietly for a time.

"Well, maybe you're right." He put his arm about her.

She drew away.

"Aw, c'mon. Don't act as if you ain't been kissed before."

She stood up abruptly.

Maury said, squinting at her, "You know, I think I got you figgered out. You'll come if I'll stay. Huh?" He waited for a reaction, then added, "Well, if that's the case you kin go to hell."

"Maybe I better go back to the house. They're waitin'."

Maury looked down at the water, and in the faint light could dimly see his white feet in the water. "Go ahead. I think I'll take a bath."

Kirsten began to move toward the end of the dam.

But Maury could not let her go. He stood up, too, and followed her. He caught her by the willows. He asked, suddenly daring, very urgently holding her close, "Kirsten, why don't you take a bath with me?"

102

"What?" She jumped away.

Again he placed his hand on her. "Aw, now, don't snap off my ears."

Kirsten shook him off angrily.

"Well, okay, sister, okay. But I'm gonna take a bath right here in front a the dam." He began to loosen his overall suspenders.

"It'll be awful muddy there," she said abruptly, curtly.

"Well, at least it'll be deep enough to cover my ankles."

Kirsten pointed south. "There's a better place half a mile down."

"How deep?"

"'Bout two feet. I used to go wading there with Tollef."

"Sand?"

Kirsten nodded.

"Come, show me."

She hesitated.

"Come."

Kirsten turned then, and together they walked along the stream below the dam.

The sound of the water trickling beside them was the sound of tiny stones falling on taut wires. The short grain whispered near them. The bare limbs of the willows were as white as flour. The few leafy branches were purple dark against the sky. The headlights of a passing car on the highway a mile away pierced the night with long, weaving, slanting shafts of yellow. A thin film of blue outlined the entire horizon.

Kirsten pointed to a bend in the stream. "There," she said. "Water digs in a little there, and right below it the sand's piled up."

"Comin'?" Maury asked again, his voice persuasive. He had felt her trembling near him.

103

Kirsten held her breath. "All right," she said, finally. But she waited for him to undress first.

Maury, pulling off his shirt and loosening the side buttons of his overalls, quickly saw her intent. "I think I'll have a smoke first," he said slowly. He felt a few tufts of grass beneath his feet. "Here's a good place to sit. Come." He drew her down, holding her shoulders as she sank with him. "There." Then he took out his cigarette makings and rolled a tube of tobacco with meticulous care. He lighted it. In the glare of the match flame, he glanced at her eyes. "Go ahead," he said. "Go ahead. Don't wait fer me."

Kirsten shook her head.

Maury laid his cigarette carefully on the ground. He loosened one of her suspenders, and then, slipping the other down, loosened her blouse and drew it off. Nervous suddenly, he muttered, "Why! you don't wear one a them breast halters, do you?"

Kirsten pushed his hands away and finished undressing herself.

Maury trembled as he picked up his cigarette again. Seeing her body silhouetted against the stars, he felt a sudden, great craving for cigarette smoke. He puffed deeply, staring at her.

Kirsten moved toward the water slowly and then dipped her feet in it. She played her toes in the water a moment and then went in. She looked upward and then stretched, her breasts lifting.

Maury threw his cigarette quickly into the water then, and tore off his overalls. In a moment he was beside her. He reached out to touch her. He ran his fingers over her smooth skin lightly, hardly touching her, as if he were touching something holy.

Kirsten drew away from him. She settled slowly into the water. She gasped when the water filled in beneath her armpits and came up over her breasts.

Maury stood looking at her and then settled beside her. He put his arm over her shoulder.

She permitted it to rest there for a moment and then drew away from him again.

He followed.

She took his hand then and held it in her hands. She pressed it nervously.

He reached for her.

But once more she drew away.

Giving up the chase, Maury settled back into the water. He stretched out his feet and let the water run over his body.

Presently he rubbed his body energetically, splashing his face and snorting a little. He dipped his head under. Then he turned and splashed her face, trying to touch her breasts with the same motion.

Kirsten laughed and then she shot water into his face by skimming the flat of her hand sideways over the surface of the water.

Maury fought back.

The water sparkled between them.

Then Maury raised his arm, pointing. "Look," he said. "Look. There's the moon. Just coming up."

Kirsten turned.

An enormous blood-gold saucer was slowly being shoved up over the rim of the earth by an invisible force. Silhouettes of distant trees were etched against it thinly, like the scrawls of a child. The northeast heavens became yellow and bright. Stars faded above. The saucer expanded. It swelled. Raised. When the disc was almost free of the earth, the lower part clung to the dark horizon for a moment like a drop of water clinging to an object before it parts. Then the moon drew the reluctant part into itself and the yellow-red orb rose slowly.

He sat watching it, breathlessly. Slowly the prairie lighted. The willow thrust up in distinct dark strokes against the sky. He turned to see what effect this prairie glory might have on Kirsten.

Kirsten was playing. She had lifted a palmful of water and was now slowly pouring it, watching the thin silver stream thicken into a deep gold.

Maury took her in his arms.

"No," she whispered.

"Please. My bunny. My bunny little cottontail. It's all right. I won't hurt . . ."

"No!"

Maury pushed his nose into her hair and breathed deeply. He whispered her name. "Kirsten. Kirsten. My bunny little cottontail."

Kirsten trembled. "If I knew . . ."

"Knew what?"

"If I knew you'd stay."

Maury hesitated.

She went on. "If I knew you'd stay. I don't like to have a baby alone by myself. I'd like to have him see his pa."

Maury drew a sudden breath. For a moment he had the feeling that he was about to fall into a chasm. He steeled himself, hardened himself against her.

She looked down, as if she were blushing. "You don't have to marry me. Just so you'd stay."

Suddenly Maury leaped to his feet and carried her to the sand below.

Some time later, when his mind cleared, he swore. He drew away from her with a sudden distaste. He went over to where he had thrown his clothes and fumbled in the dark for them. He muttered to himself. "I'll be a bastard, I will. I'll be a bastard. I'm just the guy to pull a stunt like this! I'm always forgettin' myself. I'm such a goddamn fool!"

Kirsten sat on the ground, looking at him imploringly. "Wait! Wait!"

Maury jerked on his clothes roughly. He swore under his breath. It had come to him. If he stayed another moment, he would be trapped for the rest of his life, trapped in a land of slow death. Dust and death. And loneliness more pervasive than any he had ever experienced on the road as a bindlestiff. Trapped, and possessed by an utterly helpless feeling of being unable to stop the unraveling of life and of the earth beneath it. He started hurriedly toward the farmyard.

"Maury!" Kirsten called.

Maury ran on.

Kirsten stood up, naked, and ran a few steps after him. "Maury! Maury! Wait!"

But Maury went on. When he came to a rise in the land, he turned, and saw that she had fallen to the ground, a white mound in the moonlight.

Maury ran swiftly over the half-burnt grainfield. He remembered he had hung his shoes on the lane fence and ran back to get them. He leaped swiftly over the barnyard gate and then, as he came toward the house, saw Pa and Ma Thor still sitting on the steps.

He stopped, breathing hard. He stared at them. The gold light of the moon brightened their gray hair into silver. He hesitated. They had so few moments of happiness. He stared at them, and suddenly realized that here was the future picture of himself and Kirsten.

Then he walked up to them, and Ma Thor stirred and asked, "Why! where's Kirsten?"

"She's comin'."

Pa Thor blinked, remembered, and then asked, "Say! that dam still there?"

Maury growled, "Yeh, it's still there, all right." He went inside the house. Both Ma and Pa Thor came after him.

"What's happened, son?" Ma Thor asked. "Where's Kirsten?"

Maury picked up his bundles and started for the door.

Ma Thor ran before him. She blocked his way. "Son, there's something wrong!"

Maury cried, "I didn't hurt your girl none. I just wanna go. Let me go."

"Son!"

The word cut like a whip. "I can't help it! I only know I got to get out of here. Right away. I'm . . . I'm . . . let me go!" He pushed Ma Thor roughly aside.

Pa Thor called. "Son? Son?" His voice echoed over the yard.

Maury ran swiftly, and, gathering himself into a short, mincing run, sprang from the edge of the gully. He reached half way up the other side. His guitar twanged in his arm. He crawled up the remaining distance and gained the road. He strode south, then west.

His footsteps beat hard on the gravel road. He tried to keep from thinking.

The moon rose steadily. As it lifted into the heavens, its gold steadily faded to silver. It shrank. The stars faded near it. A meteor cut a wide, irregular gash across the southern sky.

Maury stumbled on. His feet slipped sometimes in the rough gravel. Occasionally, when his foot dropped into an unexpected dip in the road, he felt his belly muscles jerk.

He walked a mile before he heard a motor drumming on the soft air of the prairie night. The sound came sweetly to him. He stopped to listen. His grim face brightened. He adjusted his suspenders and brushed his clothes. He pulled his cap around to give himself a happy-go-lucky appearance. He remembered to smile.

But the car went by.

And others went by. The old days had come again, the old days of waiting and waiting, of building up artificial smiles every little while.

After the sixth car had passed him without slowing at all, Maury knew he would not catch a car that night. Cursing a little, he hurried his steps, lengthening them over the gravel road, following the turn in the road toward the west, hurrying on toward Long Hope where the night freight would run at two in the morning, and go chortling and rattling west to the Black Hills.

Several hours later, a train whistled north of him. He ran hard to the summit of the next long swelling rise. Reaching it, he stood looking north, his breath short, afraid that the train he would see would be the night freight.

And then, there, at last, he saw it. There was a shaft of light creeping swiftly over the land. An orange glare exploded directly behind the source of the light where the fireman coaled the engine. White smoke curled through the brief, orange illumination. He looked along the train. There were no lighted coaches. It was the night freight, all right.

Disgusted, Maury swore and dropped his bundles on the edge of the road. He sat down, hung his feet over the shoulder of the highway and rolled a cigarette. He lighted it and puffed until his fingers, trembling from the exertion of hard running, quieted.

Soon his thumping heart quieted too, and he looked out over the land.

In the moonlight, the land was lifeless. It was as endless as endless silence. The prairie stretched mile on mile to the horizon. No insect life stirred in the night.

The slight knolls lay like stones. The earth was dead. It did not breathe. Its nostrils, the plants and the animals, were dead, choked by the dust.

Maury crunched his teeth. He rubbed his hand roughly through his hair. He cracked his foot roughly against the hard ground. The dust bowl was hell.

And, as always happened when he took off a little time from his wandering to muse a bit, his mind teemed with images and memories. He was haunted by old faces and old times. He had never been able to forget his father's last despairing days on earth. Or his mother's wretched life of slavery, which, like her body, had gone up in dust. It was always bitter to think of them.

But more so now. For there had come a new Pa and a new Ma into his life. Looking at the other side of the ditch, as if it were a frame for a picture, he saw Pa Thor and Ma Thor, saw their faces of just a few hours ago when they'd questioned him, round-eyed, about his going. "What happened, son? Where's Kirsten?" and Pa Thor's wretched, wailing, "Son? Son?"

He shook his head. But the ghosts were vivid. They were persistent. There they were, across the ditch, caught pictured in those tufts of weeds. How very much like Ma was Ma Thor! How very much like Pa was Pa Thor!

They were such good people. Such stubborn, lovable, childish people. They had given him board and room. Room they had plenty of, but the food must have been worth heaps of gold to them. He had taken their food, had eaten it. And then he had taken their daughter and thrown her onto the earth and taken her like a wild bull. Compared to them, what an animal he was!

He jumped to his feet. He grabbed up his bundles and started a few steps westward again.

Then he hesitated. He thought. Then, abruptly, he wheeled about and started back toward the Thor home.

He stumbled on through the early morning hours. It had begun to lighten a little in the east. He hurried. The gravel crunched beneath his rapid feet. Sometimes a sharp stone dented the sole of his shoe, bruised his foot.

He waved an arm as he went along. He began to mutter. "Yeah, it was a dirty trick, all right. A dirty trick. A helluva thing for a guy by the name of Grant to do."

The gravel squinched beneath his hard beating legs. "Well, I missed the goddamn train anyway. I'd a had to wait a whole day anyway."

He sniffed the night air. He coughed, cleared his throat, and spat to the side of the road. "It was a dirty trick, all right. Ruining a nice girl like that. Poor kid." He sniffed, and spat again. "But if I'm stayin' a while, I'm ignorin' her. I'm not laying my hands on her. I don't want to get tied down to this. Wimmen are worse than glue." He muttered along to himself. "I'll stay a couple a weeks, that's what I'll do. A couple a weeks. Two weeks won't make or break me. If there's a job for me in the mines, it'll be there when I get there two weeks from now too. An' in the meantime, I'll give the family a little lift."

He strode on, nearing the farm again.

"But by God, now that I'm stayin' they gotta listen to me, too. I got some ideas about that farm. An' old Pa Thor's gotta listen to me, or else. I got a plan."

When he came to the house, it was still dark, though the gray in the east had risen a little.

Ma Thor was up. When he entered the door, she looked up questioningly. He snorted a little, embarrassed, and then, laying his bundles beside the cot, muttered, "I . . . I been out fer a kind of a long walk." He rubbed his nose. "Well, it's late. I better get some shut-eye afore the roosters crow."

Ma Thor nodded her head, and then got up and went to the back room where the family slept. As she opened the door, he caught a glimpse of Kirsten standing in her nightgown. But before he could turn his head away from her, she had turned away. It was Kirsten who began the ignoring.

VIII

MAURY WAS FIRST OUT OF BED. He dressed quietly and slipped noiselessly outdoors. The early sun was faint behind a gray, riding dust. The rain of the previous night had vanished as if it had never been. He drew his cap deep over his eyes to fend off the gritty wind. He entered the barn.

The seven rascally pigs boiled into sudden, snorting activity when he came in. They rushed outdoors through the pighole, one above the other. Maury noted with quiet satisfaction that, though they were thin and gaunt, they were all lively.

He walked, then, through the cowbarn and opened the door to hunt for the cows. They stood near the water tank with the two horses. They turned their heads slowly and stared at him as he walked toward them. Maury looked into the tank. It was empty. Gray-green moss lay in dry flecks on its bottom. He began to work the cattle pump. The handle fell limply. He set up a series of short, quick jerks. After a long effort, the handle became heavy. And soon, a thin trickle of rusty water poured into the tank. The two cows and the two horses lowered their heads into the tank and eagerly slupped at the few drops. The sound of their sucking breaths grew on his ears. He pumped faster. The rusty stream cleared a little, became yellow-gray, and swelled. The animals kept the bottom dry with their wild slupping. For ten minutes, Maury pumped furiously. The animals drank avidly, leaning over the tank, sometimes raising a leg to get closer to the bottom.

Then, suddenly, the handle became limp in his hands

113

again. The pump gasped. Maury tried a few more strokes and then helplessly let the handle fall. The two cows and the two horses looked at him imploringly. Their eyes were dumb and soft and brown.

Maury walked to the cows and felt their teats. They were almost dry. The family was almost out of milk. He rubbed his fingers over the backs of the cows. And then, impulsively, he leaned over and smelled deeply of their red hair. He stroked them and then quickly walked across the barnyard to the feeding racks. He stepped over the fence and examined the haystack. It was mainly a pile of Russian thistles, cut when green. In it were a few tufts and strands of stray grasses. Maury guessed Pa Thor had cut and raked this mound of prickles last year just before the real heat had got to his hay and grain-fields. He found a fork and threw over a few forkfuls to the cows in their feedbunks. He watched the cows chew the weeds gingerly. He saw many sores along their lips. Apparently the tumbleweed pricks were festering.

Then Maury took a short turn over the fields. The corn was almost gone. There, to the left of the creek in a low fall of the land, a few rows of young corn were still standing. These could be cultivated. With some rain they would make good corn. But the rain would have to come today or the moisture they had had last night would only, as he had predicted before, serve to fry them.

The grainfields were a little better. Here the growth had been thicker than in the cornfield, and each blade served to protect the one next to it. Maury nodded. The grain could be good . . . but again, only if there was rain.

As he went back to the yard, he stopped at the house-yard pump to get water for the sow. He watered her and then went toward the house.

114

The wind was rising, and Maury pulled down his cap. He peered sideways under the visor as he walked across the yard, thinking about his plan. He entered the house quickly. He fixed on a good smile.

Kirsten was at the door, but he did not look at her. The two weeks ahead would be full of downright work. "Where's Pa?" he asked, when Ma Thor emerged from the back room.

Ma Thor trundled toward the stove to start the breakfast. "He's gettin' up. Always takes him a little time to thaw out in the mornin'."

"Well, he'd better get up. Can't be lazin' around on a farm."

Just then the back room door opened again and Pa Thor stumbled out, blinking his eyes.

Maury smiled, and settled on his cot near the window. He rolled and lighted a cigarette.

Presently the coffee was ready, and what little breakfast there was, and they drew up to the table.

Maury turned to Pa Thor. "Well, Pa, how's the leg today?"

Pa Thor, sipping his black coffee, smiled craftily. He rubbed his knee with his free hand. Then he looked out of the window. "Is it cloudin' up again, fer godsakes?"

"Huh? What do you want clouds fer?"

"Well, I dunno. We could use a shadow."

Maury laughed, and puffed on his cigarette.

Pa Thor pushed his chair from the table and, groaning, reached for a shoe. He lifted a foot over the knee of the other leg and slowly drew on the shoe. "What's up, son?"

"Well, Pa. It's this way. I got to figurin' last night. An' I've decided to stay for two weeks. No more, no less. Let's see. It's Friday today, huh? Well, two weeks from today I'm pulling out fer the mines. If there was a job fer me there today, there'll still be a job fer me there two weeks from now."

Pa Thor let his shoe fall to the floor in astonishment. "Two weeks, son?"

"Yeh. That's right. But . . . but, there's some strings."

"Money?"

"Hell no. Money? Who the hell cares about money? Huh! No, I'll make a deal with you. I'll work like hell fer two weeks here. Cultivatin', and . . . something else. I got a plan I'll tell you about in a minute. Two weeks. I'll take no pay. Just grub and that cot there. At the end of the year, if you make some cash, you kin send it to me in the Hills, at the regular hired hand rate. If you get dusted out, I'll chalk it up to experience. How's that?"

Pa Thor stared, and then reached for his shoe on the floor. But his back was too stiff and he jerked himself off the chair. He fell. He sat on the floor, cursing his back.

Ma Thor scolded him and got up to help him.

But Pa Thor pushed her away, still cursing. He staggered to his feet. He gripped Maury's shoulder. "Son, I'll . . . I'll . . . that plan, what is it?"

Maury puffed on his shortened cigarette, sipped at his coffee again, and then slowly crossed legs. He felt Kirsten's eyes upon him and then felt a flush rising along his neck. He coughed. "Well, it's this way. Actually, I don't have much hope fer rain. So, the corn an' the hay an' the grain is doomed. But you got some pigs there, seven real little jiggers, an' it's them I'm thinkin' of. If you kin keep them alive, there's hope. Now, how much grain you got?"

"Well, not enough fer all the animals."

"I thought so. Well, you could sell the sow fer grain." He paused. "But, what I'm really gettin' at is the greens."

116

"Greens?"

"Yeh. Animals, and humans too, need greens. An' I thought that if you was to plant a patch a greens, some radishes, an' lettuce, or some such, an' you'd water it, an' keep it goin', why, you could keep the pigs healthy. An', a course, yourselves too."

"Go on, son. Sounds like you're gettin' at somethin'."

"So, if you was to dig that cattle well deeper out there, an' could get a lot of water, you could keep the greens agoin' all summer, come hell or high water."

"Well, now . . . Well!"

"Plant the greens right here between the barn an' the house, an' the privy an' the toolshed an' the feedbunks. There's a little windbreak there."

"Well, now . . . well, now . . ." Pa Thor had finished putting on his shoes, and now he filled and lighted his pipe. "So, you think we won't get any rain?"

"No."

"An' the rain we had last night, that ain't much?"

"Why! I could make more water than that myself!"

Pa Thor laughed. "Well, the idea a the greens sounds good. We could use some green grub once. Be good to go out to the privy once more an' know you're goin's worth the time."

"Pa Thor!" Ma Thor scolded again.

The men chuckled together. Then Maury asked, "Say, how deep is that well?"

"Forty feet."

"That all? Holy smokes, man, that ain't deep atall. Think you could dig her down?"

"Sure."

"How about gittin' Ol' Gust to do it?"

Pa Thor's face became sly. He nodded toward the women. "Ask them."

Maury turned to Ma Thor. "You won't mind if he

comes? We need the water bad."

She looked down and shifted uneasily in the chair. "Why no. If we need the water, why sure."

"We do. You won't go back on us if we get him here fer a week? He'll sleep here too, you know."

Ma Thor faced Maury and looked directly at him. "I ain't never yit stood in the way a menfolks as was workin' to make a livin'."

"Good."

Then it was Ma Thor's turn to become sly. "Where you gonna get the seeds for the greenings?"

Maury shrugged. He looked at Pa Thor, who also shrugged.

Ma Thor waited a moment. She picked at the edge of the table with her long red fingers. Then, with a secretive smile, she got up and went into the back room. After a few seconds, she came back with two small salt-sacks. She laid them before Maury.

Maury opened them. "Why, seeds! Radish an' lettuce seeds! Millions of 'em!"

She nodded, and looked down, and flushed with pleasure. "I saved 'em."

Maury jumped up. "Well, let's get goin', Pa. I tell you what. There's another thing I noticed. You ain't had a bull on top a them cows fer two years, have y'u? Look. Why don't you take the horse an' wagon, an' load up them cows, an' try to find a bull on the way from here to Sweet Grass, an' get 'em bred quick, an' then hire Ol' Gust. All in one trip."

"Why, I could do that."

"Sure. An' if they should drop calves an' you ain't got the feed, why, you kin kill the calves fer veal, an' use the milk fer yourselves." He paused. "An' while you're gone, I'll fix a little barbwire around that patch where we'll plant the greens. Then I'll plant 'em, an' water 'em

118

from the house well."

"No! No!" exclaimed Pa Thor. "Don't touch that house well. There ain't much water in there, either. Just a few drops in it. An' I always keep that water fer the house. That's the wimmen's well."

"All right, all right." Maury remembered that he had earlier watered the sow from it. Next time he would know better. "Let's get the lead out then, Pa."

IX

FROM THE FIRST, Maury had success with the greens. In a little more than a week, without the aid of water, they were up, poking their little seedling sprouts through the surface of the ground. He was a little puzzled by their energy. He wondered where they got their growing moisture. But he was sure of one thing. He knew that as soon as they hit a new water vein in the old cattle well, the greens would make it. And the pigs.

The first day they pulled up the pump and the pump rods, and cleared the well-casings of fouling matter. They set up the derrick and the horse-drawn powerjack and started the drill down.

They were down three feet below the old depth when Ol' Gust began to shout.

"What's up?" Maury called from where he was driving the horses on the powerjack.

"We hit water!" Ol' Gust roared. "That blasted water's here all right."

"No!" Maury ran over quickly. Trembling, he helped Ol' Gust and Pa Thor pull up the drill bucket. They examined the contents.

Ol' Gust took off his old straw hat and slammed it on the ground. He scratched his dirty gray hair. "Sand, son, sand. We're gonna have a helluva time now. The danged walls'll keep fallin' in."

"But there's water," Maury said.

"Sure, there's water. But there'll never be more'n about three or four feet of it. An' you'll have to use a sand-point to get it out."

"Let's try to go deeper," Maury suggested.

They went down another eight feet. But the drilling went slowly. The walls continued to cave in until an empty crater, eight feet wide and eight feet deep, had formed beneath the last well-casing. The level of the water did not rise.

Just after dinner, when Maury had taken a moment to water the growths, he heard Pa Thor and Ol' Gust burst into another roar of cursing behind the barn.

Maury ran toward them. "What's the trouble now?"

Ol' Gust swore and slammed his straw hat to the earth again. "Oh, I was a damned fool again. I dropped a wrench down there."

"That's too bad," said Maury. "A good wrench?"

"Well, it was a little dinky old wrench. Had it fer about twenty years. But that ain't nothin'. What's bad is that that blasted thing fell right where the augur takes its bite. An', a course, fouls the point."

Maury squinted thoughtfully. "Well, hell, pull out the point then."

"But the damned wrench slips off it every time. Won't come up with it."

Maury forgot his greens. He peered into the dark cavern, thinking. "Did you try to hook it yit?"

"No."

"That wrench got a hole in the handle?"

"Yeah, but yellow toads an' snake bites! Tryin' to thread that hole with that hook, an' down in that well there, why! huh! it'll be like usin' a poker to fish up a needle outa a man's stomach!"

Maury grinned a little. "Well, let's give it a try anyway. Can't stop now."

Maury replaced the augur with a hook and then slowly let the square drive rod sink into the well. As it slid through his hands, wet slush from the rod bubbled around his fingers. When the hook reached the bottom of the well, Maury carefully, though blindly, steered it around until he thought he felt a pressure. Then he waved to Pa Thor.

Pa Thor slapped the lines over the horses. "Git!"

"Easy now," Maury cautioned. The rod turned slowly. Then Maury jerked the release lever and the rod came up slowly. He peered into the darkness.

Ol' Gust stood sweating and snorting beside him. "You didn't get it, huh?"

"No," answered Maury. "No. But we'll try again."

Ol' Gust picked up his flapping hat. "I should never have come out here. Never. I knew I was a goddamned fool to start this."

"Take it easy, take it easy, partner," Pa Thor said, trying to calm him.

Ol' Gust stamped around the opening. "We'll never get it out, I tell you. We'll waste a summerful a days just ploughin' around fer that goddamned wrench!"

Pa Thor rubbed his leg. "Aw, it won't be that bad."

Ol' Gust roared. "Any fool knows we'll never get it out."

Maury said tersely then, squinting, "All right, Ol' Gust, if you wanna pull out an' let us sit here, git!"

Ol' Gust grunted and scratched his head. He stared at the dust lifting and veiling the land. "Well, hell, I didn't mean . . ." He reached in his back pocket, looked over the yard to see if Ma Thor or Kirsten were around, and then started his bottle of Ol' Gust Special for his mouth.

"Hey, there," Maury barked. "Not here. Not while you're on the job fer me."

Ol' Gust gaped at him.

"I meant that. I'll kick yer guts in if you drink. Hear?"

Ol' Gust turned, wide-eyed, to Pa Thor. "He the big shot here now?"

Pa Thor looked to one side, smiling a little.

"Is he?"

Pa Thor nodded.

Ol' Gust put his bottle away, untasted. "What a bunch a dried-up peanuts!" he grumbled to himself.

Maury was firm. "That's all right. Grumble all you want. I promised the wimmen somethin' when they agreed to let you on the yard."

Ol' Gust began to stamp around. "Of all the bloody nerve! Y'u say the wimmen . . .?"

And now Maury began to smile too. He nodded.

Ol' Gust shook his head. "What a bunch a deadheads! Lettin' some fool wimmen run 'em like that. What a bunch a willies to run around with!"

"Later, Ol' Gust. After we're done. Then you can rip an' snort an' drink all you want. Hear?"

Ol' Gust rolled his eyes, swallowed, and then took out a plug of tobacco. He bit off a good-sized chew. "All right, let's get to work then."

Maury dropped the hook again. Slowly the rod turned as he searched. Releasing the lever, he pulled up.

He tried again.

He tried ten times.

Finally Maury said, "Well, there's only one way out."

"And what's that?" Ol' Gust asked, chewing on his quid of tobacco.

"Fer one of us to go down on a rope, take a deep breath, an' duck under the water, an' grab the god-damned wrench."

Ol' Gust snorted. He shook his broad, deep shoulders. "Go down there? Hell, man, don't be nuts. You're too big to get down through those narrer casin's at the bottom."

"We'll see."

Ol' Gust took him by the shoulder. "You ain't, son?"

Maury nodded.

"You're cracked if you do. You'll get stuck, surer 'n hell!"

"Won't hurt to try."

Ol' Gust snorted. "Nope. I quit. I ain't goin' to be a party to your murder. Nope, we'll let the bitchin' wrench stay down there. We'll dig another hole. What d'you say, huh, Pa Thor?"

Pa Thor, scratched his chin thoughtfully. Then he looked at Maury, laughing. "Well, son, look here. If you was to get stuck down there, how would we get them pump rods back in there again? You'd be in the way."

Maury grunted. He stripped off his shirt. "Where's the rope?"

Reluctantly, Ol' Gust handed it to him.

Maury tied it carefully around his foot. He fastened the other end of it to the windlass cable. "Now. Let me down slow on the windlass. An' I'll take this other cord here down with me. An' Pa, you hold the other end. When I jerk the cord, that's the time to haul me up. Get me?"

Pa Thor nodded.

"Now don't pull up unless I jerk the line."

Ol' Gust grumbled a little and then said, "Be careful, son."

"Don't worry. I'll be usin' my head all the time I'm down there." From the edge of the cement curb he swung himself easily into the opening. He looked around at the land, peering at the dust crossing the face of the sun. Then, as Ol' Gust let the windlass slip through the clutch, he sank out of sight.

Maury watched the cement well-casings carefully. He slithered downward, brushing dirt off the sides of the casings where the debris had been accumulating for years. The pellets of dirt hit the smooth, black surface of the water below, setting up widening ripples. Twenty feet from the surface of the water, which looked like a pool of black oil, he could feel the cold begin to creep toward him. As he slid slowly down, he looked up. He saw the tense faces of the men above him. Their leathery skins were of the color of the dust above them.

The falling dirt continued to wrinkle the water below. The casings became narrower. He drew in his shoulders, folded his arms close, and emptied his lungs of air. Once an overall button hooked on the edge of a casing, and it held him up momentarily. But, wriggling, he dropped free, and passed through the narrow neck of the last well-casing. He entered the wide, bowl-like chamber where the walls had been falling in. It was very dark. Only the black water was visible. The dirt had ceased to fall and the water was as smooth as ebony. He hung, crouched above the water. "Hold up," he shouted.

"Anythin' wrong?" Pa Thor called anxiously. Startlingly, his voice seemed to bounce up from the surface of the water, right at Maury's feet. "Anything wrong?"

"No. I'm just sizin' her up."

"What?"

Maury thought a moment. Then he realized that, though he could hear them with extraordinary clarity, his own voice did not travel clearly up the shaft of the well. He raised his voice, shouting, "I'm just lookin' things over."

"Well, take it easy."

Maury lowered himself carefully on the rope until he had hunched his height to three feet. Then he shouted, "Lower away!" He seized the free cord and jammed it between his teeth. With his hands free, he dropped toward the black water.

The cold water came up over his feet. He shivered and clamped his teeth. He looked around quickly, frantically, at the dark wet walls. There was nothing he could do now to stop the lowering, unless he were to jerk the cord. He felt the water coming up around his chest. He shuddered involuntarily and took a deep breath. The cold water seeped into his armpits, then over his shoulders, then crept around his neck. His overall began to feel heavy. He looked up once more. The faces of the men were far away, hardly distinguishable. Faintly, he could hear the well moan like a whistle in the prairie wind.

Then the water was over his head. The cold burned his flesh. He sank steadily. He reached out two wary hands through the black water. Then his foot hit bottom. He opened his eyes in the water. He could see nothing. He reached down. Soft sand and muck slimed through his fingers. He dug frantically. His lungs seemed to swell. Quick flashes spat in his eyes. Then his right hand bumped a hard object. He reached down with both hands and pulled. It was a stone.

He had an impulse to pull the cord when his foot hit something solid in the muck. He felt. It was the dinky little wrench. He shifted his foot, bent over, and pulled it up. Then he jerked the cord.

Maury felt himself being lifted swiftly. Then his head popped through the surface. He poured out his breath, stirring up little ripples on the black water.

"Okay?" Ol' Gust called.

Maury released the free cord. "Yeah."

"Got it?"

"Yep."

"Good boy! Great work. You son-of-a-gun!"

They began to raise him. Just as he was about to enter the narrow neck of the first casing above him, his right leg jerked into a cramp, doubling him up. With horror, he saw that he would never be able to pass through.

He thought suddenly of Tollef. This was the way that he must have felt when he plunged deep into the belly of the earth, with tons of dirt and stone ready to crush in upon him if the earth trembled a little. This was the terror that had leaped up in his mind, out there in that hole in the prairie, alone, with the stifling dust drifting down, and the wind howling above. How he must have shouted, and cried, and shouted, and gradually weakened, until his voice had fallen to a faint whisper. And then a lonely death. Maury trembled.

Then he cleared his mind of fears. He rammed the wrench into his pocket and reached for the cramped leg. "Wait up!" he yelled at the old men. "Wait up!" He pulled at his leg and, when he could not straighten it, he bent his other leg to push on the cramped leg's foot. But his left leg was too near a cramp to make the maneuver. The leg throbbed with sharp, ripping pains. He thought, "Well! Now I'll really have an excuse to rub my leg more than Pa ever did."

Maury looked around quickly. He shouted. "Pull up a bit."

His head and shoulders and hips squeezed into the casing. He placed his hands behind his back against the wall and forced his body forward. He pushed his cramped leg ahead until the knee hooked underneath the edge of the cement casing.

"Pull up!"

The ascent began. Maury pushed desperately. Slowly the leg bent downward until the thigh was in a straight line with his body. The edge of the hard cement casing cut his overall and bruised the skin over his knee. Muscles seemed to be ripping out by the roots. Then the back of his heel touched the other side of the casing. Slowly the leg straightened. Conflicting muscle impulses rippled painfully. Then the leg was in the casing, ring-

127

ing with agony. The coarse cement walls ground through
the overall and into the flesh.

Maury looked up. The two faces were staring down
at him. Maury laughed, nervously. "You two birds up
there look like a two-leaf clover."

"You all right?" Pa Thor called anxiously.

"Sure. Keep pullin'. What you waitin' fer, time?"

Ol' Gust spun the windlass by hand. In a moment,
Maury came out, wet and shivering, as slimy as a
drenched rat. He staggered onto the curb. His leg buckled
and he fell to the ground.

"A cramp!" ejaculated Ol' Gust.

Maury pulled the wrench from his pocket. "Here she is."

X

THE BIG WIND LAY DOWN in the south. It lay watching like a great cat. Maury could feel it, eyeing the Thor farm and its few morsels of human flesh.

Each day he expected it to strike again. But each day, instead, the Big Heat came, and burned the land with a bright and furious glare of blistering sunlight. The growths withered, and fell, and slowly blackened.

During the days, while the sun was scorching the outside of his body, Kirsten's behavior burned him on the inside. All the while he hobbled about the yard, slowly working out the kinks of the cramp, she offered no word of consolation, revealed not one whit of interest. Slim as a willow, and serene, she went about her chores, ignoring him as though he were an ordinary hired hand. She fed the pigs and watered the greens. She milked the two cows. She brought lunch to the men. Not once, even by uncertain eyelash or lip, did she betray the fact that she had ever loved him in the willows.

Nor did she show any excitement when the drill hit a boulder seventy feet down, breaking the drill-point and ending the well-boring for a time.

Maury considered her. Four times that he could recall she had shown an interest in him. She had come down to look at him in the ditch that first evening. Her voice had faltered the time she sang, "Hallelujah, I'm a bum." By the dam she had admitted that she wished he would stay. And later that same evening, by the willows, she had tried to call him back.

He snorted as he reflected on these incidents. In none had there been real evidence of love. He wondered what she had seen in him, and which of his features she had liked. Brooding over these matters as he worked with Pa Thor and Ol' Gust at the well, he determined to pick the lock of her heart before he left for the Hills.

And yet, he cautioned himself, and yet, if he was to cut cleanly away from the Thors, he must not get too curious and touch her again.

Sunday came, a day of rest. The sun began to burn the moment it glared over the eastern horizon. The very air had the heat of a stove.

All morning Maury was silent, morose. This was the day he had decided to leave. He barely greeted either the father or the mother at breakfast, and did not allow himself to show any interest when Ma Thor announced that Kirsten was not feeling well and would not get up for the day.

He brooded. Leave-taking became more difficult as the minutes passed. Pa Thor's kind, soft face musing over his pipe confounded him.

He lighted a cigarette and then got up from his cot. He strode back and forth across the room a few times and then, turning to Pa Thor, finally said, "You know, Pa, what I can't figure out is how you can live in all this emptiness without goin' nuts."

Mildly startled, Pa Thor took his pipe from his mouth and looked at Maury, shaking his head. "I dunno . . . I never thought much about it. This is the only place I've ever lived. It's all I know."

Maury nodded. He paced. "Sure, sure. I know that. But, by God, I know that I, personally, can't live here. I can't live where it's empty. I need growths. I need corn an' grain an' animals an' people around me. I think there must be something wrong with people that kin live in the Dust Bowl without goin' nuts."

Pa Thor sat up straight. His eyes narrowed, wrinkling his brow. "What do you mean, son?"

"Well, the way I see it, only empty people kin live in an empty country, people empty in their soul. Me? I'm full a life, an' got to have life around me."

Ma Thor, who had been reading a religious magazine, looked up anxiously.

Pa Thor slowly and thoughtfully refilled his pipe. Then he lighted it. "Are you sayin', son, that we're shaller people?"

"Oh no . . . I don't mean . . . I mean . . ." To hide his face, he puffed on his cigarette.

"I think I know what you mean," said Pa Thor, standing up, his body straight with dignity. "You don't need to apologize."

"Well, I meant that you people should get out a here!"

"Never mind, son. I understood you the fust time."

"Well, ain't it true?"

Pa Thor took a step toward the back room and then, turning, asked, "Son, down there in Oklahoma, there where you lived, it wasn't always empty, was it?"

"No. No, it wasn't." Maury drew furiously on his shortening cigarette.

"Well, it wasn't always empty here either."

Maury sobering, thought a moment. He took another puff, and then tossed his cigarette into the stove.

Pa Thor pointed to the window, pointed to something far away. "Son, if you was to go back to Oklahoma now, couldn't you see, if you was to close your eyes, the land full a milk an' honey again, like the Bible says?"

"Sure. But such dreamin' is fool's gold."

Pa Thor shook his head, still pointing. "Son, when I look out a that winder there, I kin still see this land as it's been. They say it's a dust bowl now, an' maybe it is. But I can close my eyes and see the golden bowl it's been. There's been gold corn an' wheat an' hay an' buffalo grass in the fall, an' gold pheasants an' cows an' women, all gold. It's been full a gold. I can see all that. This land ain't empty fer me. It's the only land I know. It's been full a gold before an' it'll be full a gold again. I know."

Unwillingly, Maury found himself moved by the talk. He nodded, and muttered, "Yeh, it was full a gold, all right. Even the cottontails had a little gold in their white tails then. A shine to 'em."

"What, son?"

"Nothin'."

Pa Thor paused, and, lowering his arm and puffing on his pipe, said, "You see, I can remember all that. An' I'm waitin' fer it to come back. An' so I'm not an empty man. Don't ever say that again." He paused once more. "I ain't never yit, not ever, ordered a man from my door. But talk any more like that, an' I'll have to send you on."

Maury flushed. He fired inside. "But it's the truth, Pa! It's the truth! An' anyway, I personally, I can't see them dreams fer this godfersaken country. I can't see 'em. I think you've been blinded by fool's gold."

Pa Thor paled. His brown suntan took on a purple hue. He trembled.

Maury turned quickly and took out his cigarette makings and nervously rolled a cylinder of tobacco.

Pa Thor said, "You been sayin' you're goin' to a job in the Hills?"

"Yes."

"Well, I think this is about as close as you'll ever get to it."

Maury whirled around so abruptly that a few grains of tobacco spilled from the cigarette in his lips. "What do you mean?"

132

"I mean, your job will always be a hundred miles ahead of you."

"What?"

Pa Thor said, very deliberately, "You're one of those fellers that kin do a lot a talkin' as long as the job is a hundred miles away, but the minute you get near it . . ." Then he turned and, ignoring Ma Thor's outstretched hand, went to the door of the back room.

Maury shouted, "So! I can't get a job in the Hills, huh! Well! we'll see about that! We'll see."

Pa Thor said, ignoring him, "Ma, this is supposed to be a day a reverence. I . . . come. Come, let's go down and visit the Graysons. His wife has been ailin', an' we ought to pay our respects an' regards."

Ma Thor hedged, "But . . . uh . . . kin the horses travel ten miles in this heat?"

"Comin'?" Pa Thor asked curtly.

Then they left. Left without another word. At the last moment, when it had looked as if Ma Thor, hesitating in the door, might have had a kind word for him, Pa Thor had angrily called out, was she ready? And then she had left, silent.

Maury stomped about in the kitchen, pacing from the cot to the table. He muttered. He brooded. To quiet his nerves, he played a few tunes on his guitar. But when he remembered that Kirsten was still at home in the back room, he returned the instrument to its case.

Presently, Pa Thor's words began to turn in him, and to cut him. And, even though there **was** danger of sunstroke and blindness, he made up his mind to go today. He packed his guitar carefully, wrapping a few extra sheets of paper around it to protect it against the heat. He rolled up his clothes and then, when he noticed that a pair of socks and a workshirt were missing, went into the back room in search of them. Ma Thor had probably put them there after she had washed them. For a fleeting second, he glanced at Kirsten lying on her cot by the window. She seemed pale, he thought. And feverish. He left the room without a word. He finished packing his two bundles.

And then, for the first time, he noticed that he still had not lighted the cigarette in his mouth. He laughed to himself, nervously. He struck a match and puffed a while.

He brooded.

He had provoked Pa Thor into giving him an excuse to go. But there was still Kirsten.

This time, before he entered the back room, he knocked.

There was no response.

He entered then, and strode toward her.

She turned slowly from the window to look at him.

Maury paced by her bed. "Kirsten, I'm goin'."

She stared at him and raised herself on her pillow.

He was pleased that he had stirred her. "Yes, I got to go now. I . . . Well, I'm gettin' on my own nerves here . . . an' I guess, your Pa's too."

"That was your own fault," she said, quietly.

"You heard?"

She nodded.

"Well, maybe. But I just can't understand how a person kin live here with all this emptiness . . . unless he's empty hisself. An' . . . I ain't. I'm full a life. I got to be where there's things goin' on. Growin'."

She did not respond.

He looked at her, and then paced again. "Why don't you say somethin'?" he asked sharply.

Her blue eyes opened a little.

"You never say nothin'. Nothin'. You never say nothin'. You look at a man an' never say nothin'. By God, it . . ." and then, a curse having passed his lips, he suddenly realized that lately she had caused him to curb his swearing a little . . . "it drives me nuts. Why don't you say somethin'? Don't just sit there an' stare like a cow."

"What's there to say?"

"Aw!" he roared, and paced on, back and forth, raging. "Wimmen . . . Chr . . .! If you'd only talk so a man could figure you out, figure who you was. Every woman wants somethin'. Some want men, some want homes, some want gossip. Every woman wants something. What do you want?"

She said nothing. A curious illumination fired her eyes.

He paced. He thought. Suddenly he stopped and pointed. "You're holdin' something from me, ain't you?"

"No."

"Sure?" He looked at her with suspicious eyes.

"No."

He grunted. "Well, at least you kin say 'No.' "

A momentary feeling of compassion for her arose in him. "What's wrong that you're in bed here?"

"Oh . . . nothin'. Just feel a little weak is all. Food didn't agree with me, I guess."

He snorted. "An' no wonder. Feedin' a woman, feedin' people pickled tumbleweed pricks, ain't buildin' health, I kin tell you."

Her eyes opened with surprise.

He laughed a little. "You thought I didn't know that you wimmen were pickin' young green Russian thistle an' picklin' an' cannin' 'em, huh? Well, I did. Yeh, an' I laughed to myself when your Ma served them an' called them Chicago Hot. 'Makes the meat tasty,' she said. Huh! An' we didn't have meat that day." He laughed again.

Once more she became silent.

135

"Well, woman, what does ail y'u?"

"Nothin'."

He reached forward to touch her brow. Before she could draw away, he touched her. "Say," he exclaimed, "you got a fever!" He looked at her. "An' here I been ravin' at you as if you was fit to fight." He puffed his cigarette stub once more and then squeezed it between his fingertips and dropped it into his pocket. Then, "Could I get you some water?"

"If you wanna."

He snorted a little, and brought cool water in a sweating pitcher.

She drank from the pitcher, and then, setting it aside, resettled in bed.

He looked at her faded blue dress. He was pleased to see her out of overalls for a change. "Kirsten, tell me, what makes you tick inside? What do you want?"

"I . . . what are you talking about?"

"I mean, what do you want to do? Every man, woman an' child wants to do somethin' someday. Even the animals has such kind a dreams."

She turned her head slowly and looked out of the window. Her eyes looked afar.

"Babies?" he asked, remembering the pigging sow and her ministering.

She turned to him again. "What else is there?"

He stared at her. "Babies? Just babies?"

"Yes. What else is there? Kin you think a anything else?" Her eyes half closed as she talked on. "I love little things, little just-born things. Whether its pigs er chickens er calves. The more they need help, the more I like 'em. Poor little things."

"Babies!" he exclaimed. "So that's it." Instantly he had a vision of her, twenty years from now. She would be entering a church. Behind her would come young, pret-

ty daughters, fluttering their new hats and handker-
chiefs. Outside, still talking, as all the men did before
they went inside to sit with their families, would be a
patch of young sons, young, strong, blond-haired bulls of
the land. The image cut him. How could he, or she, ever
hope to raise such a family in this desert?

He leaned forward suddenly, and said softly, though
intently, "Kirsten, come with me. Come with me."

"Where to?"

"The Hills. Anywhere. Anywhere. Come with me. An'
fer godsakes, leave this dusthell here. Come."

She shook her head. "If this land is good enough fer
Pa and Ma, it's good enough fer me. Me, I'm stayin'
here." Then, with a mocking light in her eyes, she asked,
"Are you sure you kin get a job in the Hills?"

He stared at her; then, instantly, he left her and went
into the kitchen and picked up his bundles from his cot
and closed the door loudly and started down the hot,
burning gravel road for Long Hope. Come hell or high
water, he would catch that freight tonight.

XI

IT WAS TEN O'CLOCK that night when, exhausted from the heat and the day-long walk, he arrived in Long Hope, carrying his bundles. Fumbling in his pockets, he discovered he had just a half dollar. He was tempted to use part of it for tobacco, but his hunger for food was greater than his craving for nicotine, and he bought a meal in a dusty, broken-down cafe that did not offer the customer a glass of drinking water.

Having eaten, he walked toward the railroad yard. He learned that the night freight would come through at two in the morning, just as Pa Thor had said. He felt sleepy, and, looking around, decided to lie out on the open prairie to the south. To the north of the tracks, except for the depot, lay the silent town. He walked out about a hundred feet, far enough away from the yards to escape the notice of yard cops, yet close enough to hear the train when it should come stamping in from the east. He fell asleep instantly.

He slept soundly, so soundly that he did not hear the freight come in. And when he did awaken, lying flat on his back, his head on his bundle, he was horrified to find that a rattlesnake had crawled against his overall pant-leg and lay nestling its slimy body against his right thigh. He did not need to see it, or feel it, to know that it was a deadly rattler. He remembered all the old stories of the many farmers who had awakened in the morning to find that a rattler, to warm itself in the night, had crept in beside them in their blankets.

He cursed silently. He fumed. He was not frightened, for he knew that the rattler would not strike as long as he lay quiet. It would strike only in self-defense if it felt something move in the dark. But he would miss the night freight. He sought through his mind for a plan to rid himself of the snake. He lay very still.

He resigned himself. He sighed. Yes, he would have to wait until morning, until the sun rose high enough to warm the numbed reptile and send it on its sinuous way. And that would be at least seven o'clock, a good five hours after the freight had left. Why! the freight would have reached the Hills by that time.

Slowly the train clanged a hundred feet to the north. He listened to the shout of the brakeman. He watched the lanterns weave the magic of the trainmen's language in the night. He heard the steam hissing. He heard the powerful pistons driving the wheels on the rails. In the black night the engine resembled an enormous boar, eyes flaring, ears up, and nose driving and rooting into the earth.

Maury's mind whirled on itself like a dog chasing its tail. He must find a way of escaping his visitor.

He wondered if he could rid himself of the creature by lighting a match. Maybe he could warm it sufficiently by lighting a handful of matches. It would be easy to light them without moving. He remembered that once, when he had leaned over a railing, and had slowly slid along it, a pocketful of matches had popped into flame, searing his thigh flesh; and on the very thigh where now this snake was sending off its chills against his skin. Yes, he could slowly rotate a batch of matches in his fingers until they popped into flame. He had, he thought, about a dozen sticks in the pocket of his shirt.

But he decided against the matches. The sudden glare of the flame would startle the reptile. And that was the one thing he must avoid.

He brewed. He listened to the freight train switching

cars. The headlight of the engine in the night was sharp on the land. It caught the sides of the empty grain elevators in great gold pillars of light. Above, the stars twinkled serenely.

He lay very quiet. He was pleased that he could be so calm in the presence of the deadly rattler. Life had not yet beaten him down to make him a whining dog.

Then he remembered that once he had seen a man playing with rattlesnakes in a small village along the Highway. This fellow had been as calm as God. He called himself Rattler Jack.

Rattler Jack had snakes running over his ears and lying coiled in his cap on his head, and emerging from his shirt pockets, and crawling in his pants pockets, and twining up his legs.

Rattler Jack was the most fearless and deliberate man Maury had ever seen. Rattler Jack moved like a snake himself. His gestures reminded Maury of the first time he had come into the barn to help Pa Grant harness the horses. Pa Grant had said, "Maury, always let a horse know you're comin'. Always. An' he'll never kick you. An' never move quick-like. It scares him." And then Pa Grant had made a sudden move at Maury and Maury had instinctively jumped. "See?" Pa Grant had said. "See? You got scared too, didn't y'u? It's the same with horses. And one thing more. Be a man around 'em and they'll be horses around you. Now go to work."

And Rattler Jack had lost part of his tongue. One time, to impress a particularly snake-frightened Dakotan, he had put a snake's head into his own mouth. And then, to emphasize his point that snakes could take a joke, he withdrew the snake and stuck his tongue out at it. And, in that gesture, he made his one mistake. The tongue had moved too suddenly. The snake, mistaking it for a darting enemy, had struck.

Without blinking, Rattler Jack had dropped the snake in a basket, whipped out his jackknife and quickly cut off the tip of his tongue. And then, his mouth geysering blood, had run to a doctor half a block away.

Recalling the story now, Maury puckered his tongue. He shivered. The movement disturbed the snake. Maury sucked in his breath. He lay very still. He prayed that his leg would not tremble, and tried to keep his thoughts away from it. A thought might cause it to stir.

The train clanked. It whistled once. Twice. Maury groaned. The whistle signalled the end of the car switching. In a moment, the train would start up for the Hills.

Then he had an idea. Cautiously, with his left hand, he pushed his bundles away from his body. He began a very slow movement of withdrawal, as if he were once more harnessing jittery horses down in Oklahoma. He remembered to breathe quietly and regularly. He moved his left foot over, his right, his head, then drew his hips away.

When the support of his body gave way, the snake tumbled a little. Maury's lips trembled. But the snake did not uncoil. It slithered a little and then lay quiet.

Again he angled his legs and head away from the snake, and then withdrew his hips.

The snake did not move.

But by now the train had started. It screamed twice again, and then snorted loudly, starting up its first getaway strides.

Again he moved his head and legs and then drew his hips away. Again the snake rolled a little, but did not strike. Maury moved more surely, and faster. When he was two feet away from it, he suddenly bounded to his feet and, grabbing his bundles, leaped away.

He ran stumblingly; his legs were weak with trembles. Gradually, he gained control of his thigh and calf

141

muscles. The banging guitar hummed against his legs.

For a few steps he gained on the freight. At the angle he was running, he was ahead of the last six cars and the red caboose. Then he was ahead of but four. Then three. Two.

He was within ten feet of the tracks when the last car roared up close to his running feet. His shoes crackled on the cinders along the edge of the railroad ties. He leaped forward, but missed the ladder on the last car. He tumbled and twisted a little and cracked against the oncoming caboose. It hit him hard and spun him around and threw him violently away from the train. He fell on his side and rolled over and over. The ponderous wheels rolled close by.

When he got to his feet again, the train was hooting far to the west.

He shook his head. He picked up the bundles the caboose had knocked from his hands. He stepped across the tracks. He walked toward downtown.

He muttered to himself as he stepped along. He recalled that he had had strange dreams as he had lain on the prairie with the snake against his leg. The touch of that snake through the cloth had inspired them, no doubt; just as the dust bowl, and hunger, and cruel, hard eyes, and whizzing cars leaving him standing on lonely corners, all these, had given him nightmares. And it came to him that he could not remember having had, in the last four years, a single happy dream in his sleep.

XII

In the moonlight, Long Hope looked a haunted place. He stood listening a few minutes. Only two street lamps burned on mainstreet. Now that the noisy freight had left it, the town was mysteriously and overwhelmingly silent.

Suddenly, a motor spattered its exhaust into the still night. He heard the gears mesh, heard the tires spin on the gravel highway. And in a moment, the headlights of a car bent down over the road. Well, he thought, well, maybe here is a little luck at last.

Maury waved his arm as he blinked his eyes in the blinding light.

The car approached him rapidly. Then the brakes screamed and the car stopped beside him.

Maury walked up to the side of the car. "Howdy, sir."

"Hello. Where you goin'?" a warm voice asked.

"West. The Black Hills." Maury observed the car and guessed it to be a '26 Dodge. He looked at the grinning youth. Maury judged him to be a farmer's son, just now successful in love.

"Hop in. I'm goin' down the road a piece. A couple a miles."

The Dodge barked sharply. They drove on.

The young man said, "You farmin' hereabouts?"

Maury nodded. "I was."

The young man turned the wheel back and forth a bit as he drove along. Sometimes he spurted the motor and laughed when the exhaust pipe roared. He said, "No, there ain't much to farmin'. I'm glad I quit. Me, I work in a gravel pit fer the Guv'ment. There's a little livin' in

143

that yit . . . as long as they need roads to get across here."

"Say!" exclaimed Maury. "Say! they got any need fer any extry help?"

"Naw," said the young man, half-rotating the wheel. "Naw, they're about to close down."

Maury settled back in his seat.

Soon the young man slowed his car. "This is as far as I'm goin'."

"Thanks," said Maury, picking up his two bundles. He opened the door and stepped off the running board.

"The highway turns north a mile west a here," the young man shouted.

Maury nodded. "Thanks, fella."

He walked on.

After a time his feet tired, and he sat down to rest and to smoke a cigarette. He took off his thin-soled shoes and rubbed his toes, and his calves and his legs and his back. He rested a while and then slipped off to one side and onto the ground. He fell asleep again. He was very tired.

The Milky Way became a wisp of white flimsy and then disappeared. Slowly a late quarter moon faded in the east. The lights of dawn crept over the horizon and stole along the ridges and the roofs of empty deserted houses and barns, and bare bony windmill frames, stole along like timid white mice, silent, secretive, and furtive.

He lay in the road ditch. A few ants crawled over his pantleg. Dust from passing cars covered his clothes and face with a fine grit. He slept heavily, with his mouth open; and when an inquisitive ant, its feelers quivering and vibrant, ran into his red dry mouth, he suddenly exploded a cough. His face turned deep red as he fought to rid himself of the fierce itch deep in his windpipe.

Finally, with a desperate hackle, he brought it out. He moistened his tongue with saliva, then slowly wetted his palate. He looked around and remembered where he was and how he had come. He fell asleep once more.

Later, when Maury lifted his sleep-thickened face, the sun was just beginning to push its bold red nose over the rim of the earth. The sun looked like a drunk coming home from a night of revelry.

Maury stood up wearily, limb-stiff. He watched the white lights along the surfaces of things turn yellow in the sun, watched the purple dark of the valleys fill with the spilling flood of light.

Presently, very hungry and thirsty, he picked up his bundles and began to walk on. Tumbleweeds rolled across his path. The wind rose and moaned in the wires and in the hollow steel fenceposts. The telephone wire hummed above him. A vulture flapped overhead in circles, greedily inspecting a row of chalk-white bones in a gully.

Soon Maury saw that during the dark of the night he had wandered off the Highway. He stopped in the middle of the road to look back. He could not see the turn-off from where he stood. He meditated. Finally, with a toss of his shoulders, he set off again, going west.

Later, he saw a sign on the road ahead. Hurrying toward it, he read: *Bad Lands, Two Miles.*

Quickly, Maury looked west. And there it was! The real Bad Lands. Two slim peaks jutted up over the next rise in the land. To his left, a deep arroyo broadened as it ran zigzagging westward. Big Foot Hill staggered upward behind him.

Maury walked on, to the brow of the next rise. Beneath him lay a painful beauty, a poignant desolation. The sun struck slantwise across the spires and peaks.

The dusty colors were suddenly ripe. Lonesome crags sat observant.

He was fascinated by the spectacle. He forgot his hunger. The morning sun, still low in the east, created thousands of little shadows in the weird mudrock formations. In the valley, the larger shadows became purply black.

He lighted a cigarette and then sat on a rock to study the fantastic land. His imagination, made alert by a ravening stomach and morning ecstasy,conjured strange shapes and forms.

There to the left he saw little castles and minarets, exactly as he remembered them from pictures in his grade school history and geography books. And tottering candelabrums, rising and gleaming in the clear blue sky, with faint hints of flames above them.

He stared. He stared so long his eyes began to water a little. He saw, through the moist film, an hourglass half-filled with running sands.

And there, down there, deep and to the left of that shadow, there was a lamp, a lamp hauntingly similar to Ma Grant's lamp with its bright reflector. He shook his head. What a wonder this was! Now he understood why Pa Thor had always become dreamy when he thought and talked of the spired land.

Maury studied. He saw slim blue needles and shining pins. He recognized the eyes and ears and noses of friends he had not seen for years.

Down ahead, why! there, there was the tortured breast of a woman! And there, a bulging muscle of a man! And a gaping mouth!

And tables and chairs of pine. And old brown clocks. And pink-yellow gravestones. And green trees. And houses. And barns and cultivators and plows and scrapers and horses and cows. Why! there were enough things here for God to set up housekeeping.

He mused and dreamed. There to the right was a cloud. It floated gently above a dark patch of shadow. Its top was a bowl of whipped cream. It floated above the earth.

He lifted his eyes and saw, a mile west, a haunted city. A city burned. A city of ashes, its buildings gutted and its streets everywhere strewn with furniture lying awkward now in the open light of the sun where strange fire-crazed people had carried them.

He wondered. He remembered now, too, that Pa Thor had spoken of the Bad Lands as a place filled with history, with the bones of beasts a million ages old. He blinked his eyes. The tumbled ruins and rocks became the fearful old animals again, rumbling and grumbling among themselves.

He had an impulse to play his guitar. But he was hungry, too. He wrestled with the two impulses for a few moments, and then gave up the idea of music. He got to his feet, and trudged slowly down into the contorted valley.

There was a time, long before the Great Glacier in the north began to creep down the sides of the earth, that the country in the valley before the Black Hills, now known as the Bad Lands was an enormous tropical swamp. It lay along the north shore of an ocean that shrank and became merely the Gulf of Mexico. This great swamp wriggled with gargantuan life, with the oreodon, the brontosaurus, and tyrannosaurus rex. In it, savage-toothed triceratop struggled with wallowing dinosaur. The hollows and bogs and puddles were loud with the wrestling of treacherous reptiles. There were sounds made then, and echoes, that no man's ear has ever heard. Millions of the most monstrous bodies, caging but the very feeblest sorts of mental light, died every day for thousands of centuries. And filled the bottom of the huge swamp with their bones.

And then presently, the earth began to cool. The first Great Glacier began to form and to draw up the waters from all the oceans. The swamp dried. The last few monsters struggled, succumbed.

Then the saber-toothed tigers reigned over the drying land. They hunted the giant pig, the tiny camel, the mountain sheep, and mountain goat. The giant rhinoceros played in the few remaining puddles. The three-toed horse galloped swiftly over the knolls and down the sides of the brown-green bluffs.

The land dried still more. It became covered with short, sparse grass.

Endless days of hot sun finally came. It cut the grass and the roots of the grass and left the meat of the land open to the wind. And then, when the abrupt, ripping rains came, they slashed at the raw meat of the earth. Gullies soon ran east and south. Gullies deepened. Sometimes boulders and chalky layers of sand and clay mudrock were uncovered. The hard rains and the hard dry winds cut away at the soft meat and left the glistening bony spires.

And then the saber-toothed tiger died too. And the three-toed horse, and the camel, and the sheep and goats. They laid down their bones on beds already heavy with the skeletons of saurians.

Soon buffaloes ran from the mountains in the fall. They ran from the cold and snow, and came cropping, their damp, black noses eagerly smelling what little sparse grass was left. After they passed by, the ground was harsh with short stubbles and torn roots. And the sun came, burning the roots. And the winds blasted at the layers of sand and the blades of grass.

Later the rains ceased entirely. Drought made the subsoil brittle. And veils of volcanic ash, anciently sprayed over the land, flowered into brilliant colors in the hot sun: purple, pink, blue, and yellow.

Each spring, after the snow had melted and the water had run off and the winds had cut the land again, the settlers and cowboys and curious people found the bones of ancient barn-sized creatures.

The land became celebrated. Tourists came to view this once holy land. They studied it momentarily and then rushed on, assuring themselves that after this they could find nothing new under the sun.

When the tourist trade became profitable, the Government, which had made of this land a national park, granted a concession to a family to set up a curio-and-eat-shop. A winding spur of road was cut and graded down into this wound in the earth. It was graveled. And then great flocks of travelers came in the summer, cackling and chattering ecstatically over their find.

It was down this spur that Maury walked. It wound in and out through the gutted valley between the yellow and purple and pink strataed spires, and then suddenly dipped into the earth. Then it spread fanwise into a deep, two-acre flat. Here, half-way along, deep in the hot hell of the valley, he found the curio-and-eat-shop. A sign announced that pop and coffee and lunches were on sale. And chips from fallen saurians and meteors.

Ten cars of various models were parked before a railing. Behind them, a hard path ran up to a wide log door.

Maury walked slowly with his bundles, studying this new place. His muscles were stiff. His once-cramped thigh throbbed involuntarily. His body felt as dry and as cracked as the baked earth beneath him. He walked stiffly toward the shop. He stopped. He sat down on a stone near the shop with his two bundles stacked neatly beside his legs. The yellow dust and sand were almost too bright for his eyes. He shaded his face with his hand. He sat pondering, his elbow on his knee. Sometimes he wiped the sweat from his face. He lifted his trousers away from his leg to let the air touch his sweaty skin.

He was very thirsty. Gas rumbled in his belly. He looked at the cafe a long time, thinking of a way to get free food. He worked at a story he could tell the proprietor. He wanted the story to be honest.

He examined the waiting cars minutely. The back seats and the running-boards were piled with clothes and camping equipment. There were no rides for him in these cars. Tourists abhorred bindlestiffs.

Maury took off his hiked cap, carefully ran his fingers along the leather band, pulled at a bit of lining and put it on again, pulling down the visor with a firm jerk. He muttered a few words. Once he swung his arm in a circle. He wiped his face again and snapped the sweat drops off his fingers with a quick flip. He crossed his legs and then uncrossed them. The taut denim of his pantlegs was wet from sweat.

There wasn't a breath of air. The hot sun beat down. The glistening mudrock spires made a noise like talk.

Maury finally stood up and crossed the yard, following the hard path to the door, carrying his bundles, one under each arm. He opened the screen door and stepped inside.

A young couple sat at a table to his left, while two elderly, dignified men stood at the cigar counter talking to a tall man with rolled-up sleeves and a jutting Adam's apple. Off to one side, another room was half-filled with tourists.

Maury looked at them sharply, and then turned to scrutinize the man with the Adam's apple. This was the proprietor.

Maury set his bundles on the floor by the door respectfully and then took off his cap to brush back his hair. He felt the eyes of the two old men and the proprietor hard on him.

A folder of colored cards on a show case caught his eye and he went over to look at them. He acted as if he were absorbed in the pictures and then, moving to his left, looked at a tray of odd stones and a few meteors. He fumbled with them.

The three men resumed their low talk.

Presently, Maury thought of a plan. He walked across the open space and sat at the counter. He studied the menu carefully, attentively running his fingers along the price list. He shifted his feet a few times on the railing beneath the counter and then ran his fingers through his hair. He rubbed the palm of his hand over his unshaven chin.

When the two dignified strangers stepped outdoors, the tall proprietor came up. "Yes?"

"Howdy," began Maury. "Well, look, mister. It's this way. I ain't got the price of a meal on me, but I need the grub bad. Real bad."

The tall, gray-eyed man stared at him. A frown soured his face. "This ain't no relief station."

"Well, could I have a glass a water then?"

The hard-eyed man stared at him stolidly. He swiped at a fly and finally moved. "Yeh, I guess I kin let you have that."

Maury drank greedily. "Another glassful?"

The man filled his tumbler again. Then the man wiped the counter carefully, cleaning up glass rings earlier customers had left. A dour old woman passed along with a tray of hot food for the tourists in the side room. Suddenly, the man asked, "Come a long way?"

Maury nodded. "Walked all last night."

"Where you from?"

Maury fumbled for his cigarette makings. He hesitated, then said, "Well, my home is really in Oklahoma. At least it was four years ago. An' since then, I've been lookin' fer work."

The man's eyes narrowed. "Work? Real work?"

"Real work." Maury lighted his cigarette and took a deep puff. "Yes sir. Real work."

"Work any these last four years atall?"

"Oh, a little. A little all over. A little job here, a little job there. Now I'm headin' fer the Hills."

"I see."

"Yeh, heard there was jobs in the mines there."

The man stared at him and began to chew on a match he had found. His eyes were still narrowed.

Maury's eyes narrowed, too. "Was stayin' with a Dakota farmer fer a couple a weeks. Helped him fix a dam. An' drill a well. When my time was up, I come on. An' then lost my way here."

"Well, didn't you get your wages?"

Maury looked down. He affected a sigh. "Well, the goddamned farmer was broke. An' I just couldn't take what money he had."

The proprietor studied him a moment, and then hearing the honeymooners scrape their chairs as they got to their feet, walked toward the cash register. When they had paid him, the proprietor came back and said, "Well, you better get a move on. I can't have fellers lookin' like you hangin' around in here. It drives my trade away."

"Why? What fer? You can't lose. They can't very well stop anywhere else, kin they?"

"Well . . . I don't like it, is all."

Maury nodded. "Okay. Say, you ain't got some dishes to wash or something? That your wife that just went by here with that tray a food?"

"Yeh."

"She looks tired. Maybe she could use some help."

The tall man stared at Maury and then said abruptly, softening a little, "I like the looks a you, but I don't know. Ellie!" he called.

His wife came in from the back.

"Got any dishes fer him to wash?"

She studied him. "No."

"I'm terrible hungry, lady, an' I'd sure appreciate a little work so as to get some kind a handout."

"No."

The tall man suddenly walked into the back room and then came out again.

"Sure, there's dishes to wash, sure." He waved to Maury. And then, as Maury walked past him, he said, out of earshot of his wife who had gone on to the side room, "Wimmen! When wimmen get into business, they get a heart a stone!" He led Maury through a low door into the kitchen. "You kin lay your cap on this table. Them your bundles out there by the door?"

"Yeah."

"I'll stick 'em behind the counter fer you. Now you kin tackle that stack a dishes there. If you do a good job, there'll be a cup a coffee in it fer you." He walked out, leaving Maury with a sphinx-like, male Chinese cook.

Maury worked carefully, swiftly. He finished the dishes. Then, finding a broom, he swept the floor carefully. With a dirty mop, he scrubbed the floor. He dusted the windowsills, and the tops of the stoves, and the cabinets.

Then he called the proprietor. "I'll take that cup a coffee now, mister."

The man stared at the neatly stacked dishes and then stared at the floor. "Well, I'll be damned! Damned if I won't be damned! That's cleaner than my wife er cook ever had it." He stood staring at the floor. "Come on. You earned your cup a coffee all right. Go sit out front where you was before an' it'll come right up."

Maury walked out front and read a newspaper until the tall man came out. Then Maury dropped his paper in surprise. For there, before him, the tall man, now smiling, had set out a plate of bacon and eggs. A cup of coffee steamed to his right. Maury swallowed, choked. He was speechless.

The tall man was pleased to see Maury's embarrassment. "Well, hell, eat it."

Maury fell to hungrily, gratefully. After a while, he asked, "Many cars come through here?"

"Some."

Maury chewed rapidly. "It's hard to catch a ride with them birds."

"Yeah, I suppose."

"I been wonderin' if you could do me another favor. Ask one a them that stops here if he kin give me a lift. Tell him you think I'm a square guy."

"No. No, that's somethin' I never do. That's against the house."

"Okay. But I'd sure appreciate it if you would, though." Maury chewed on a juicy strip of bacon. Saliva welled in his mouth. Then he said, "Huh! Guess I looked kind a crummy, comin' in like I did."

The man laughed. "Well, you didn't look like a new dollar bill."

Maury laughed with him. They became friendly. Maury said, "My name's Maury Grant."

"Fellers around here call me Beanpole Pete. Pete." He wiped his thin forehead and then folded his arms over his gaunt chest.

"Well, I didn't know what to say or ask," Maury explained. "But I just had to eat. Just had to eat somethin'."

Pete smiled, and then said, seriously, "Well, I can't

blame you, an' I see your point okay. But you can't blame me fer bein' suspicious at first. I got a tight wife back there." He paused. "Though I hain't no fool either. I can't be givin' stuff over the counter an' gettin' nothin' back." His voice began to whine. "I did it fer a long time, an' I'm goin' broke. An' if I do, my wife'll run out on me, I guess. Why! a Guv'ment feller wanted to know, what the hell, why ain't I makin' dough here? I says to him, 'Get them damn bums off the road an' then I'll show you.' That's the way it is, you see."

Maury nodded. " 'Course, you got to have money comin' in."

"Damn right." Pete waved his arm and then leaned forward. He looked over his shoulder to see whether his wife was near and then said, "You know, I get so discouraged when I see you fellers comin' and' goin' day after day. . . . So discouraged! Once in a while I get a half a notion to tell the Guv'ment they can go stick this concession they give me here, right up their fanny. Really! I mean it!"

Maury squinted and nodded.

The thin man sighed. "But I got to make a livin', so I never do."

"Yeh, you got to make a livin', at least."

"Sure. You see how it is. But, I'm still mad, see? Sometimes I just get so goddamn mad, I don't give a damn who I'm mad at, an' so I throw out the bums. The wrong guys, see. Fellers like you."

"Yeh, I kin see that," Maury said, sipping his coffee. "I kin see that. Yit, the fella that gets hungry, all he knows is how hungry he is. That's all he thinks about. He don't see you, the real you. He just gets sour inside at everybody. Why, today, I was jus' thinkin', when I was settin' out there on that hot stone there in the sun, I was thinkin' that, by golly, pretty soon they'll be chargin' us fer air. Why! I'll bet you that they'll be chargin' us a good round dime fer five sniffs. Sure!"

The two men looked at each other, mutually admiring the picture Maury had drawn. They laughed together. Pete said, "Sure, there's that side of it too. I kin see that."

Then Maury asked soberly, dipping his bread in the coffee, smacking his lips over the warm food, "Do you think bums kin ever be real people agin?"

Pete studied the question carefully, looking at the floor, scraping his free foot back and forth. He looked out of the window. He pursed his lips. "I dunno," he said finally, "I dunno. They's been hurt pretty bad. Some a them will. Some won't. Some ain't got enough brains to work. Some ain't got enough guts to steal."

Maury sat back. He had finished his meal. He fumbled for his sack of tobacco.

"Funny world," Pete ruminated.

"What's gonna happen?" Maury asked, looking ruefully at his empty sack.

"I dunno. Say, you out a tobacco?"

"Yeh."

The man considered, looked at his tobacco stand, and looked at Maury, wrinkling his brow in thought.

"Never mind," said Maury. "Never mind. I'll get a job an' then I kin smoke."

Pete looked at him. "Naw," he said, "naw, I can't let a smokin' man out a here without tobacco. Here's three old Bull Durhams. Real old an' dried. Never sell 'em here anyway. Tourists buy tailor-mades these days."

"Aw," mumbled Maury.

"Take 'em. An' here's a tailor-made too."

"Aw," said Maury. He slid off his seat. "Thanks." There were tears in his eyes. He squinted.

XIII

THE DAYS OF A FULL WEEK WENT BY.

He combed the Hills for a job. And always, as he hunted, he heard part of himself laughing, tauntingly, as though it believed he would never find work.

He had come to expect turn-downs. They were inevitable. He had aimed himself at distant jobs so often without success that he wondered whether there would ever be a real chance to work again. Each locality had its own unemployment problems. Like Omaha and elsewhere, the Hills were alive with lean men looking for work. And behind the grilled windows of employment offices the owners became alert for unrest and the power of the unions. Thus the nearer he came to a town where he thought a job might be, the less he was sure that it would be there. Pa Thor might have been right that a job would always be a hundred miles ahead of him.

It was an aching solace that the green life in the Black Hills gave him. It seemed ironic to him that a land filled with stately ponderosa pine and western white spruce and red cedar and juniper close to the ground, should have no job for him. And that the lofty hills weighted with hackberry and ironwood should have no shelter for him.

At night, weary from walking, and hungry, he crept into the resin-running pines and lay down on the needles, and shivered in the hill cold. He stared up at the stars. He heard the wind whispering in the conifers. He wondered on his existence.

One day he managed to get past the guard at the gate

to the mine. He had to argue with the man for a long time, and even after he had finally been passed he felt there was still a danger of being called back. He had seen the guard go into the small warming-hut to telephone.

Another guard, standing near a door marked *Employment Office,* studied him, too, before he let him pass.

And then he was in the presence of the personnel director. "Howdy," said Maury. He took off his cap, and brushed back his hair with his fingers. He took a seat across from the man. He hooked his cap on his knee, placed the bundles on the floor beside his chair, and looked up into the eyes of the man. The man was short, and his smile, meant to disarm, contrived instead to warn people of danger. The skin on his face was extremely flexible. He had learned to arrange his face for the needs at hand. His manner reminded Maury of a salesman's deadly friendliness.

Maury studied the man's blocky shoulders. Looking up, he saw a football letter tacked to the pine-panelled wall and, beneath it, a portrait of the man taken years ago. The calf-like eyes in the portrait were unsteady.

Maury blinked. The fellow had been talking to him. "What?"

"I said, you looking for work?"

"Yes."

"There's nothing here. I'm sorry."

"No?"

"No." The man pushed an application blank toward Maury. "But, if you want to, you can fill this."

"Will that get me a job?"

The man shrugged.

"That's what I thought," Maury said, squinting, and he tossed the paper back to the man. "That's what I thought. I've filled them out before. I always say, if a boss's got a job fer a fella, he won't fuss with no papers."

The man's face hardened. "You know a lot about looking for work, don't you?"

"Yeh."

"Where's the last place you worked?"

"In Dakota, on a farm."

"Why didn't you stay there?"

Maury grunted. "Mister, if you was to be eatin' a piece a the last chicken leg in the world, would you like it if I come along to help you eat it? Would y'u?"

The man blinked.

"No, mister, you wouldn't." Then, "I've looked everywhere for work. If there ain't no job fer me here in the Hills, there just ain't any jobs anywhere atall fer me."

"That's kind of unpatriotic talk, ain't it?"

"It's the truth."

"Huh huh," the man grunted. "Say, how'd it happen you come on here?"

"I read about the mines in the papers."

"What papers?"

"Oh, it was a paper down in Omaha." He thought a moment. "I don't rightly remember the name of it."

Maury could feel the man study his face and hands, his shirt and overall. "Ever work in a mine before?"

"No."

"Well, how come you all of a sudden want to work in this mine?"

"I dunno. I just want work, is all."

"Sure?"

"Sure I'm sure. Why, is there something wrong in my comin' here?"

The man's pale blue eyes studied him.

"Somethin' wrong?"

"You're sure you came on here looking for work . . . only work?"

"Say, what is this? Sure I come on here lookin' fer

159

work. What else?" Then, "Well, you got a job here fer me . . . or not? I'm hun . . . I got some things to do. I got to get me a room yit fer tonight."

The man stood up. "I'm sorry. There's no work."

"You sure?"

The man walked to the door and held it open.

Reluctantly, Maury stood up. He studied the face of the man. Then, shrugging his shoulders, he picked up his bundles and walked through the door, and went out and down the sidewalk and through the gate. He wondered, as he nodded to the guard, how the personnel officer behaved around dogs. It was a dead cinch that Pa Thor treated strangers better than this bird did.

Maury entered the Black Nell Diner. "Howdy."

A fat man, so blond he was almost albino, stood bent over a griddle, frying hamburgers. He looked up when Maury came in. "What'll it be?"

"Well, I think . . . well, I tell you, mister, it's this way . . . I'd like to wash some dishes for you."

"Oh, one a them kind, huh?"

The man's talk was so loud that Maury gestured for him to lower his voice. There were five other customers in the place. They looked up now, gaping. Maury said, "Well, I just thought . . . you see, I washed dishes fer a fella back in the Bad Lands, an' he give me . . ."

'Just a minute, I'll go back and look." The albino pushed his wide body through a low door and entered a shanty that had been built onto the diner.

The man did not return immediately. Maury, wondering why it should take him so long to make up his mind, suddenly heard a telephone receiver click. Then the man came back. "Well, I'll tell you, bud," he said, "you'll have to wait a bit. I . . . there ain't enough dishes to make it worthwhile washing yet."

"Who was you callin' there, fella?"

"Why . . . I wasn't callin' nobody." The fat albino was suddenly uneasy.

Maury stood up. He gathered his bundles under an arm. He glared at the albino. Then he said, squinting his eyes, "You know, mister, I got a good notion to mess up this joint."

The albino gasped. His eyes went quickly down to Maury's free hand.

Then the door opened. Maury whirled. Two burly forms loomed up. Two cops. Their stars were close and shining near him. The tall cop grabbed his arm and drew him toward the door. The short cop pushed him. As Maury went out, he caught a glimpse of the customers staring at him, with pieces of half-chewed food lying on the tongues of their opened mouths. The albino began to polish the counter absent-mindedly.

The cops walked him up to a patrol car.

"All right, bud, tell us."

Maury shook himself free of their hands. "Look, I'm from Oklahoma. An' you don't need to hogtie me." Then, "You guys horn in on a guy so fast he ain't got time to say his 'Howdy.' "

"Never mind the greetin's, bud. Tell us where you're from."

"I said it. Oklahoma."

"Why didn't you stay there?"

Maury stared at the tall cop as if he did not understand the man's stupidity. "You ain't heard?"

"Heard what?"

"How the angels a the Lord come and druv us out with a flamin' sword?"

"Oh . . . one a them talkin' guys, I see."

Maury shrugged.

"What'd you come up here fer?" the short cop asked.

His voice seemed to come out of his navel.

"Lookin' fer work."

"What kind a work?"

"Work. Ord'nary human work "

"Sure?"

"Look! I'm not in the habit a chewin' my cud twice."

"Where were you lookin' fer work?" It was the tall cop again.

"In the mines."

"Why?"

"I saw an ad in the paper."

"Where?"

"Look. You're in cahoots with that hardcase boss over there in the mines. Ask him. I told him all about it."

"Where'd you see this ad?"

"I dunno."

"Huh. So. Are you sure you was only lookin' fer work?"

"Sure."

"Sure you wasn't thinkin' a some other kind a work?" A sly look wrinkled the tall cop's face.

"No." Then, "Say, what the hell's wrong with this town? It got fleas that everybody's smellin' around everybody else? Why! it's like movin' in with a bunch a dawgs."

"Sure?"

Maury spat vigorously to one side. "Christ!"

The short cop now tugged him around. "Sure you wasn't thinkin' a doin' a little funny business?"

Maury only stared at him.

"You know, union business, maybe?"

Maury clamped his mouth shut. He understood suddenly. He knew now why the old wobblies and union men in Omaha had walked around like cautious dogs, as if they felt someone were always watching them.

162

"Supposin' you wasn't to get a job, where was you headin' fer then?"

"Oh-h . . . Wyomin'. I ain't never been there **an'** I thought maybe I'd give it a try."

"Well, mister, maybe you'll try it sooner than you figured on." And with that the two men suddenly seized him and searched him. And then hustled him into the patrol car and brought him to the city limits and headed him west on the Highway.

XIV

HE TRAVELED SLOWLY ACROSS WYOMING, following the Highway.

He squinted and blinked his eyes. He felt unsure of himself. He was dazed from hunger, and from viewing a land he had never dreamed existed. He crossed mountains and valleys and draws and wastes. He went down Whoopup Canyon. He crossed irrigated valleys fertile with fragrant alfalfa and fattening cattle. He crossed dry rivers: the Rawhide, the Wildcat, and Crazy Woman Creek, the Big Lightning, Little Lightning, and Twenty Mile Creek. He starved in the bowl of Goshen Hole where the land was as horribly eroded as it had been in South Dakota. He went slowly through the towns of Sundance, Spotted Horse, and Clearmont, through Rozet, Gillette, and Buffalo.

One noon he found himself a few miles below Muddy Pass, on the west side of the great, abrupt, lifted thrust of the Big Horn Mountains.

Maury sat on a rock along the side of the Highway, looking out over the edge of an enormous drop-off. He studied the torn earth beneath him. Two immense valleys, lined with balsam, spruce, and pine, came up from either side of him and joined below. Far over, a cliff staggered abruptly upward to half the height of the mountain, and then cut off into a level forested plateau. The plateau rolled evenly south a mile and then began to roll and break into hundreds of deep canyons and arroyos.

To the right, and near, alpine fir covered a dropping

scarp of rock. In the sun and shadows the bark of the fir was sometimes silver, sometimes orange, and the upper part of each tree was veiled with purple-violet blossoms.

He looked at the lupine in the draw, at the dwarfed gentians climbing the faces of rocks, at alpine sedges and avens. He smelled the mountain heath. He squinted at the green mosses and dwarfed raspberries. In the Douglas fir he observed the lichen hanging like Ol' Gust's beard.

There had been a shower a while before, and rain-drops, still clinging to the long needles of the yellow pine, made the forest a vast green mist.

He listened to the sound of stillness in the great forest.

He shook his head. He looked at his feet. Here was all this bursting growth; and here, right in the midst of it, was he, hungry and homeless.

He squinted at the running valleys. Absent-mindedly, he reached for his guitar. He began slowly, as always, tuning at first, setting the pegs; and then, presently, loosening his stiff muscles, flicking his hand. The bass chords deepened. He sang—

> *Oh! why don't you work*
> *Like other men do?*
> *How the hell kin I work*
> *When there's no work to do?*
> > *Hallelujah, I'm a bum,*
> > *Hallelujah, bum again,*
> > *Hallelujah, give us a handout,*
> > *To revive us again.*
> > *Again . . .*
>
> *I went to a house*
> *And I asked fer bread.*
> *A lady came out,*
> *Said, "The baker is dead."*
> *Is dead . . .*

165

Then he closed his eyes and intoned—

> *God tells you to work hard, live hard.*
> *God tells you to ache hard, die hard.*
> *And that's all right.*
> *But when God tells you to go to hell t'boot*
> *That's too damned hard fer this ol' toot.*
> *Ol' toot . . .*

The echoes of the rising and falling chords filled the woods and joined the never-resting whispers of the conifers. Long trailing clouds weaved thinly above him like great wreaths of lingering cigarette smoke.

Maury remembered the night he had played the guitar on the Thor farm after the rain, when Kirsten had sat listening to him, her feet in the fresh soft mud. He remembered her voice.

Then, as he strummed, an idea he had been trying to suppress, welled up in him, and gripped him fearfully. What if Kirsten were to have a baby? But before the full meaning of the thought could become clear to him, he heard the sound of a car. Thankful for the interruption, he leaped to his feet. He waved frantically.

The car stopped. It was a Ford pickup.

Maury opened the side door and leaned in. "Howdy. Got a ride west?"

"Yeh. How far?" The heavy-limbed driver's eyes were alert with curiosity. He had a lean, brown face. Maury guessed his age to be thirty.

"Well, I'm headin' fer Ten Sleep, an' then north," Maury said.

"Hop in," the man said, after a moment of scrutiny.

The Ford started slowly at first, then shrugged into second gear, and sped down the mountain. Soon the road hopped over to the left side of the canyon and clung to it all the way down.

The sun neared its setting, and purple shadows filled

the deep holes of the earth. Piercing, slanting sunlight cut through the pines and sprayed the spruce with silver.

Both men were wordless until they reached the level plain below. Then the driver turned his head and asked, "What you got in mind to do?"

Maury's eyes narrowed protectively. "Well, had in mind workin' in one a them wheat fields up in Montana. Heard they had a good crop."

The man nodded slowly. He tugged at his wide hat. He looked out of the window to the left and then stared ahead. He had a nervous gesture, which he repeated methodically, of touching the gearshift handle with his hand and then suddenly jerking it back to the wheel. "Who told you that?" he queried.

"Oh . . . guess, I . . . well, I don't remember."

"Uhuh."

Maury studied the road. "Ain't there anything to it?"

The driver nodded, and said slowly. "There ain't and there is."

Maury kept his silence.

"There ain't and there is," the driver continued. "Where they has irrigatin', they has crops. Where they ain't, they don't."

Maury turned. "Think a man's makin' a mistake goin' up there?"

The other pursed his lips. "Well, that all depends. Got any friends up there?"

"No."

"Then you are."

Maury's face showed his disappointment.

" 'Course," said the other, "if you wanna go, I kin take you up to north a Greybull, about a hundred miles from Billings."

Maury sought for cigarette makings. "Is there anythin' up there a workin' man can find?"

167

The other shook his head.

Maury said, "I'd be much obliged if you took me that far, though."

The other eyed Maury's cigarette rolling. "Here, have a tailormade."

Maury thanked him clumsily.

The driver said, "You act like you got something on your mind."

Maury said slowly, squinting, "I should have. I ain't worked steady fer four years."

They entered Ten Sleep at dusk. Maury could hear the drum of ranch-land dance music.

The man said, "My name's Tom."

"Mine's Maury."

"Well, Maury, let's have a little bite to eat."

Maury hesitated.

"Come on. It's on my boss, see. I'm a driver fer a big ranch just over the border in Montana and I've just been south a here to look over some new breeds my boss heard about."

Maury said, "I don't like to take somethin' fer nothin.' "

"Well, what the hell? I'm askin' you to eat an' you're gonna eat. Besides, you kin take a turn at the wheel tonight."

Maury smiled.

They entered a restaurant. The ceilings were low and the woodwork and tables were made of pine logs. There was a smell of rawhide and sage in the room. An old crone appeared silently at their table.

Tom said, "Got chicken, Molly?"

Molly nodded.

"Is it good?"

Molly nodded.

Tom asked Maury, "Chicken all right with you?"

"Hell, yes!"

Tom nodded. Molly disappeared silently. Tom said, crossing his arms on the table and lowering his voice confidentially, "Molly's a nice old girl. But she never says nothin'. Never. I yit can't understand why they let her work here. She don't jolly the customers."

Maury leaned forward on his arms over the table too. "Why, what's wrong with her?"

Tom shook his head, simulating sadness. "Poor girl. Poor girl." He sighed, drank some water from his glass, and then sighed again. He said slowly, "Poor girl. She was livin' down here a ways, sheep-herdin' with her husband and two sons. Well, back in the days when the sheepmen were battlin' the cattlemen, back in 1903 er so, all a her family got rimrocked."

"Killed, you mean?"

"Killed, I mean. Rimrocked. You see, the cattlemen hated the sheep. The sheep et what little grass there was too clos't to the roots, and their sharp hooves cut the roots. An' fust thing with the wind an' sun, there warn't no grass no more. An' sheep gives the land a stink the cattle don't like, an' pretty soon there was no place where the cattle would go. So the cattlemen got mad. An' they sent warnin's, but more an' more sheepmen come. An' so then the cattlemen rode at night, whoopin', with mean dogs, an' ridin' horses and shootin'. They druv the sheep over the cliffs. Rimrocked 'em. An' sometimes the herders got stampeded with 'em. An' that's how she's lost her men."

Maury said nothing for a time. He squinted. Finally he shook his head and said, "There sure wasn't much kindness them days."

"Not a bit. It was a hard world then. Tough. An' Molly is from that time. She's still tough. She ain't said a word since. Some folks says she's layin' fer the guys that did it to open their yap. An' then she'll get her sweet revenge."

"Well, they probably'll never talk up now. It's thirty years ago. Maybe they're dead by now."

Tom shrugged.

Then Molly returned with steaming plates. Maury studied her while she set out the food.

When she left, Maury joined Tom and fell to.

Finished, Maury shoved his plate ahead and then sagged in the corner of the booth. "That was the best meal I ever et." He sighed. "It sure was." He pulled out his tobacco and papers.

"Here, have one a mine," Tom offered.

"No, I'd like a rolled now. Best part of a meal is the smoke. An' them tailors is all right, but when a fella gets used to these he don't want nothin' else."

Tom nodded.

Someone came through the door and again the sound of music and dancing came to Maury. Through the fiddles, a bass viol, a drum, and a piano, Maury could hear the clear sharp beat of two guitars.

Tom drummed his fingers on the table as he smoked. "Say, where you gonna bunk tonight?"

"I dunno."

"Why don't you take a room with me?"

"No. No, I'll find a shadow in a corner somewhere. I've been big enough expense to you. You tell me where to meet you in the mornin', an' I'll be there bright an' early."

"Well, feller, you look like a guy that appreciates things a guy does fer him. You're stayin' with me. An' I won't take 'No' fer an answer." Then, "Besides the room won't cost me more if you come."

"Well . . . all right."

Two wrinkled, spider-slow cowboys came in. Down the

street, the music in the hall had risen. The door was slow to close and Maury heard the full verse of a song—

I'm ridin' old Paint, I'm leadin' old Fan,
I'm off to Montan for to throw the hoolihan.
They feed in the coulees, they water in the draw,
Their tails are all matted, their backs are all raw.

Maury drummed the tune with his fingers. He wished his guitar were near. He had an impulse to go to the truck to get it.

Then Tom asked, a wondering look in his eyes, "Say, it ain't none a my business, but . . . you ever get hungry fer a dame?"

"Sometimes."

"How d'you take care a it?"

"Don't."

Tom jerked back a little. "No?"

"No."

"Fer chrissakes! Then you ain't . . . ?"

"No."

"Never had a soft, white woman in bed with y'u?"

"No."

Tom looked at him slyly. "Never, huh?" He waited a second, then said, softly, laughing a little. "Aw, you're a goddamn liar."

"Sure I'm a goddamn liar."

"You know, you got the looks of a guy with a big ache inside."

"Well, maybe I have."

"Best thing in the world fer that is a woman. How'd you like to go to this shindig with me tonight? An' pick up a gal."

"Out there?" Maury gestured toward the door through which came the sound of more music.

"Yeah. We're strangers, but they won't mind. Some a

171

the girls like new fellers to come around. An' maybe we kin pick up a piece."

"Not me," said Maury, suddenly a little upset.

"Okay. Have it your way. But let's take a look at 'em, anyway."

The streets were filled with cowhands and brightly-dressed cowgirls. Above, the stars were strung out through the heavens like knotted taffy. The wind was coming down from the mountains fragrant with the smell of green pine.

They neared the dance hall. Some cowboys, quite drunk, and bright in their Sunday boots and colored shirts, slouched before the door. As Tom and Maury entered, the cowboys eyed them silently, watchfully.

Once inside, Maury studied the clothes of the men and then decided to brush up a little. He went to the men's room and brushed his clothes carefully and then combed his stiff hair. He slapped dust out of his cap. He wetted his hair around his ears, and then, satisfied that he did not look like a bindlestiff, stepped into the hall again.

Maury stood watching the couples whirl by. He saw that Tom had found a partner. Then Maury saw two girls dancing together. As they passed along, they eyed him hopefully. A line of cowboys along the wall called lewdly to them, and the two women laughed nervously and skipped out their dresses and swung their hips.

Suddenly, on an impulse, Maury cut in. "Howdy, ladies," he greeted. "Now, look here. You know it ain't right fer women to be dancin' together. It ain't natural." He parted them and took the short, dark-haired girl in his arms and immediately held her close. The other girl, a tall blonde, looked at him archly and then went to the sidelines.

Maury drew the little dark one closer. She pulled away

a few steps and then, after studying his face and peering into his narrowed eyes a moment, nestled in his arms.

They danced together for a time. Then soon she began to ply him with questions to draw him out. When Maury gave her stony answers she seemed puzzled by his manner. Her darting eyes hunted in his face. She smiled oddly. Presently she closed her eyes and danced up close to him. He grinned to himself.

After a little time, she looked up. "You sure go in fer close herdin'," she said. "My!"

"Well, if you don't like it, why don't you take on one a them there?" Maury gestured toward the cowboys standing along the wall.

She drew up her nose a little. "I don't care fer any a them top-railers. I want somethin' diff'runt."

He drew her close.

The band suddenly changed tunes and instantly the dancers lined up for a square dance.

A man stood up and began to chant—

First lady swing the gent with the two tromped toes,
Now the one with the red-blue nose,
Now the one that wears store clothes,
Now the dude of the ballroom. (Swing!)
Promenade all.

Second lady swing the gent who leans,
Now the one who's full a beans,
Now the one that wears the jeans,
Now the dude of the ballroom. (Swing!)
Promenade all.

They danced on, laughing together.

"Who are you?" she asked.

"Oh, just a maverick."

"Sheep or cow?"

"Houn' dog."

"Tell me."

"Well, I'm an FBI man."

173

"Aw, chew it finer, mister."

He laughed.

Again the band changed tunes. Two of the players began to sing—

> Come to a river and couldn't get across.
> Paid five dollars for an old blind hoss.
> Wouldn't go ahead and wouldn't stand still,
> Went up and down like an old saw mill.
>
> > Turkey in the straw, turkey in the hay,
> > Roll 'em up and twist 'em up a high tuckataw,
> > And hit 'em up a tune called Turkey in the Straw.

And then the players stopped to rest for a while. Maury and the girl walked slowly to the side of the hall through the throng of laughing dancers.

"Never saw you aroun' here before," she said, still probing, as they stood near the railing waiting for the band to strike up again.

"I'm just travelin' through."

"Oh? What kind a work do you do?"

"Oh, I'm a ranch foreman for a rich guy up east. Got a ranch a couple a hundred miles north a here."

The girl stood closer. She wrinkled her face with what she thought was an interesting dimple. "Let's have a beer," she suggested.

The music had started just then and Maury, looking uneasily off to one side, conscious of his empty pockets, said, "No. Let's dance again, kid."

Then the guitars began to beat. He drew the girl near him. She followed his steps closely. They jostled each other. They puffed a little. When they happened to swing away from the others on the far side of the floor, away from the watchful eyes of the cowboys, he swung his hip hard against her.

The girl said, "You ain't asked my name yit."

"No," said Maury, squinting, "an' you ain't asked mine."

"Well, what's yours?"

"Frank Gotch," Maury said, thinking swiftly, and remembering, for some odd reason he did not understand, the name of the famous wrestler.

"All right, Frank. I'm Stella Burns. My pop owns a ranch down south a here."

Maury started. Another woman with a father who owned some land! He looked off to one side, and then danced swiftly with her.

Presently, he led her outdoors.

The yellow lights of the dance hall spread square gold blankets on the yard. He led her through the light and they entered a clump of pines. There was a smell of sweet balsam. He held her closely. She responded. He ran off with her into the dark beyond.

When they came back into the light, later, she kept asking, "What's the matter, Frank."

"Nothin', I tell you, nothin'!"

"But there must be. Don't you like me any more?"

Maury stared at her. His lips were thin and white. His eyes were almost luminous. "Christ, no!" he said. Then turning away, he muttered to himself, "I sure got euchred that time."

XV

T HERE WAS NO PEACE.

For several weeks he drifted over the state of Montana, staying a few days at various ranches where he managed to earn his board and room, bumming rides from truckers and ranch wagons, moving from irrigated valley to valley, hunting steady work, hunting a home.

Once he wandered through the Shoshone country, in the northwest corner of Wyoming. It was arid terrain, rough, and rolling irregularly, reminding him of the face of a man with dried-up boils. And wherever he saw the Indian paintbrush flaming, he thought he saw the rash of ill-kept flesh.

Presently, he faced the thousand-foot cliffs of the Shoshone Canyon. Huge sandstone fronts hung over the road like enormous eyebrows, glowering their colossal and massive ponderosities down upon him in weighty disapproval. A winding highway had been blasted through a narrow gap, and it seemed to him, as he rode into it with a trucker, that at any moment the road would slip and lose its precarious grip on the sides of the towering drop-offs.

And then they were through it, and free. He looked upon the rim of the Shoshone Dam. It lay in a valley. The mountain ranges to either side were covered by the Shoshone Forest. Here and there, freaks of nature broke the blankets of pine and fir, revealing where once tormentive volcanoes had pimpled and vexed the surface of the earth. The trucker pointed out the oddities to him: the Laughing Pig, the Camel, the Garden of the Goops, the Bear, the Goose, the Wooden Shoe, the Holy

176

City, the Devil's Elbow, the Anvil of Thor, and the Four Old Men on a Toboggan.

But there was no work here, nor on the dude ranches hidden back in the recesses of the valley.

Maury became hungrier, leaner, more worn and spent, and increasingly more restless. He still carried his guitar but his other bundle had become smaller. He was down to his last overall and shirt. He still had a suit jacket but it was worn at the elbows. His shoes were worn through and he used cardboard to protect the cracked callouses on his feet from the sharp bite of the gravel roads.

Maury began to worry that winter would find him still hunting for work. He tried to get public relief and on WPA, but lacked a permanent address to become eligible. A bitterness like rancid yeast worked in him.

He played his guitar seldom now. There was a day, though, when he sat beside a road that ran in a valley between two columning mountain ranges. He was seventy miles from any city, up in the great Gallatin Valley, west of Gray Peak. Another trucker, turning off the Highway to go up to the Hebgen Reservoir, had left him stranded there in the early morning. Not a truck or a car went by all day.

So indestructibly huge, so vast were the terrors and rages of these elements around him, now stilled into hard rock, that at first he only sensed this canyon as an oversized picture. His mind could not grasp it all at once.

When no cars came, he wandered off the Highway, sortying a little into the woods and glades. He discovered strange and wonderful flora. He saw the mountain yellow-rose, and clematis puffed up beside a stalk of antelope brush, and the beaked hazelnut running below the mountain alder. He observed, from the bank of a trickling stream, a slender stem of a birch leaning whitely over the curling waters.

Then he noticed the birds, and the range of their variety; the swift, quick lark sparrow pausing like a brown thought above him, swaying and balancing in the pure thin air with legs adangle, and open mouth asong with a soft melancholy air; and the red-breasted sapsucker barking the tree; and the crested bufflehead proudly enraged; and the whiskey jackjay whistling angrily; and the mountain chickadee calling brightly as it fluttered from limb to branch to treetop.

He was astounded by the dusky grouse; silently as a tree he stood near a brook to watch it call. Sitting upon the ground, tail spread out and down upon the earth, its wings dragging, it drew in an endless breath until it had puffed up a bag of air in its neck. Then, nodding its head, it jacked the air away, emitting strange, eery calls, clear and echoing off the granite cliffs.

The western mockingbird enchanted him. He had impulses to imitate its mimicry of other birds. If the magpie screamed, it screamed. If the jay squalled, it squalled. And always, as it sang, it turned and whirled in the air, lifting with black-and-white wings its drab and easily-camouflaged body.

Once, a bald mountain eagle beat its way along on powerful wings.

And animals—the carcajoy, the lynx, the creeping bobcat and puma, the ponderous, snuffling grizzly bear, the forest-crowned elk, and the timid, whistling marmot.

Returning, once more bending his thin soles harshly upon the gravel road, he looked up and marveled at the enormity of the huge scarps and slags of mountain basalt, and blocks of black fire-rocks gleaming in the downbeating sun, and sandstone crumbling beneath the endless, eroding weight of days.

The shadows reversed themselves. The long dark shades of the afternoon crept upon him like couchant pumas. The dark green leaves of the aspen quaked.

He cowered beneath the shadows of the crags, beneath the horror of unshaped matter, beneath the titanic and iron desolation of a ripped and distended earth that was but feebly covered by a forest. Dark, rusty cliffs topped by towers of spruce loomed over him. Magpies screamed overhead. How frozen and immobile were those once-volcanic passions and furies of the earth, in which now, his tiny passing life-impulse was caught up like a lost and pop-eyed grasshopper!

In the valley, he saw a deer scattering stones in the curve of a distant stream. The gentle creature appeared from time to time out of the deeps of the forests.

And soon he was playing his guitar, and listening to the echoes bound off the high rocks, one on the other, listening to his singly-plucked notes quivering like raw human nerves in the wilderness. He varied the sound of each of them. He listened for the note with the greatest echo. He listened for the sound that would express the full majesty of the rocks resting about him in lion-like sleep and repose. He searched for the tune that would express and drive away his loneliness—

> *Down burns the sun!*
> *And the trough in the bluff*
> *Spills over wild clover.*
> *And the shoulders of the boulders*
> *Are wide on each side*
> *With pine on the run.*
> *Pine run . . .*
>
> *Down goes the sun!*
> *And the prairie in the valley*
> *Runs full of elk bull.*
> *And the break is awake*
> *With the howls and the growls*
> *Of cat on the run.*
> *Cat run . . .*

But presently he laid his guitar aside. It wasn't the same anymore.

The afternoon of the day faltered through the blues of the evergreens. The sounds of life vanished. There was only the unceasing and unending lull of the earth. He fancied that he could hear the earth wheeling through the universe.

Then, miraculously, toward sunset, when the gold and red splashed in great streams over the mountain tops into the valley below, a car came up.

He shouted for joy. He leaped. He waved his arm frantically. He laughed. He wept. A car was coming!

When it came closer, he saw that there were two cars, one towing the other. In the first car, a coupe, sat a man and two young women; in the rear car, a touring model, an old couple with the back seat jammed with camping equipment.

"Howdy."

The young man said, as the women studied Maury with the straight-seeing eyes of a Kirsten, "This is a bad place to look for rides, bud."

"I know it."

"But I suppose we'd better pick you up."

"I'd sure appreciate it."

The young man shook his head. "This motor a mine's got quite a load already, pullin' all these women and people along, an' two cars full a junk." He shook his head gravely. "Got a long haul ahead, and sometimes we gotta go it uphill." He pondered. "Well, guess we better pick you up. Better crawl onto the turtle a the coupe back there. And hang on." Then, "Kin you hang on there?"

Shivering, for the winds of night were flowing down the canyon already, Maury said, "Yes."

Slowly the engine of the coupe growled, and pawed,

and tugged at the heavy load given it.

Maury, sitting on the back of the coupe, and facing the old couple in the crippled car behind, thought he saw the old man gesture like Pa Thor. And the old lady there, he was sure, was bent over as though work on a prairie had become too much for her.

XVI

EVENTUALLY HE FOUND HIMSELF near Billings, Montana. Every field-worker, barley shucker, and bindlestiff has at one time or another visited Billings. It is the largest railroad junction and jump-off in the Northwest.

It was evening when he arrived. East of the city there were small bonfires on both sides of the railway, each of the fires circled by hoboes.

Maury walked down the railroad between the orange fires and peered to either side. He saw a dim light. There were crudely scrawled words: *Food. Cheap food.*

Hoboes had come with bits of this and that, and had thrown it together for the benefit of all. Meals could be purchased for a nickel, if a man had it. And if a man was broke, he got his meal anyway. This was a place of giving even though those who gave had little to give.

Maury walked up to the jungle cafe and went in and asked for food.

The gray-bearded man behind the rough board counter looked at his guitar case.

"No," said Maury, "if I have to give that I'll go without."

The bearded man eyed him swiftly and then nodded. He passed him a steaming plate of cabbage and potatoes. "Bring the plate back," the old man said. "Be sure to."

Maury nodded and crept through the shadows toward the first bonfire. The fires had been built on the barren moraine to fend off the chilly Montana night. Cold air was moving in from the sandstone cliffs to the south and east. The curving Yellowstone was lively with star reflections.

Men sat around the fire, silent men, who looked into the flames, ears cocked for a freight train's whistle. Each had his own bundle and kept his own counsel. They did not notice Maury. They merely moved aside to let him into the circle.

He sat beside poets and philosophers, men who had their own way of telling about the mountain slopes and dying grass and dying people, and about morning sunrise seen through eyes squinting from hunger.

They talked, though sometimes they did not use words. They gestured, eloquently and lingeringly. Sometimes they spoke loudest and most rapturously when they sat unmoved. Their clothes spoke. Their postures spoke, cried out the unwritten and unwritable ecstasy of their suffering and hope. The language of their lives was intelligible to Maury because he lived as they did, because his appetites were blunted and whetted like theirs.

The lonely understands the lonely. The hungry understands the hungry. The cold understands the cold. And never does the cheerful one know what the lonely one is saying. Never does the well-supped perceive what the hungry one means by his intonations. Never does the well-clad understand what causes the cold one to shiver. And when one of these wanderers has been lonely and hungry and cold, all three, he becomes another creature, capable, in a moment of agony, of uttering the poem, the one word, that opens the door to a universe.

A magnate may have on the wall of his office a map covered with little flagged pins that tell him a little about the world he is struggling against. But his map is never as bitterly accurate as the mind's map of these hoboes who run across the land like lean and hungry ants. They have a pin in their minds for every kind or cruel person they have ever met. They know where the relief officials are kind and generous, kind and stingy, or hard and generous, hard and stingy. The hobo's hunger-sharp eyes are quick and true in their estimate of a man's face, his voice, his eyes, his shoulders.

And so the wanderer sits by his fire, his eyes half-closed. He dreams. His lips move. He speaks to a comrade by the fire, to a comrade whose eyes are filming with memories, who, too, is warming his heart with secret and welling images of his own anciently lamp-lighted table and chair.

The first talk they have with a stranger concerns food and where to get it. They wait for him to push aside his empty, gravy-streaked plate, wait for him to sigh over a cigarette, and then ask about it.

At last, after Maury had set aside his plate and started up a cigarette, the man next to him spoke, his bearded black face working, his thin smile hidden in the blackness. "Chuck ain't bad here. It's even got meat."

The short man across from Maury nodded. "Yeah, it's better than the meringue pie I got up at Minneapolis."

Blackie asked, "You mean, where they hand out a piece a calf-slobber along with yer cup a coffee?"

Shorty said, "Yeah. Minneapolis used to be a good place to get food. 'Ficials were hard, but they gave a guy a break. I don't mind talkin' to hard-boiled guys, because they make a man bristle up, and then a man knows he's still a man. And he kin axchilly straighten up his back fer a minute with a mad-on. But, hell, now Minneapolis's got the smilin' kind, and they ask too goddamn many questions and they don't give you nuthin' because they got too goddamn many rules."

Blackie said, "Them guys don't know a fella's movin' in strange places all the time, doin' somethin' different every minute in different places. How kin a fella remember where he's been every minute?"

A slim man on the other side of Maury, rubbed his knee. He smiled apologetically. His voice was soft, like cornsilk. He had the eyes of a farmer. "Yeh, I know about that place, too. Came through there three weeks ago. The fella smiles an' says somethin' about straightenin' out an' then says, 'Sorry, fella, but you was through here about four months ago an' you boys kin only get two meals an' a flop once a year here.' "

Blackie pursed his lips, looking sidelong at Maury. "Didn't they have a camp fer the boys there once? Where a fella could sit in the sun in the afternoon and have a respectable talk by hisself?"

Slim said, "Sure. And they gave you a few pennies if you worked, too." His voice became wistful and his eyes closed slowly.

"I wanna tell you, though," began Shorty, "take it easy in California. Hungry people there are thicker'n flies on a goddamn mince pie."

Blackie growled. "Worst place in the whole world is down south. I know. Just look at them ankles onct. Chains dug in right there, see?"

Maury followed the talk carefully.

Shorty said, "Best damn place fer help is in New York."

Slim said, "Naw, Illinois and Ohio fer me."

Blackie said, "Naw, none of 'em is any good."

Shorty asked, "Well, what's a man gonna do?" He looked at Maury hopefully.

Maury looked at the fire.

Slim said, "Funny, you walk in one a them places an' the guy looks you over. Then he says, 'Your name? When'd you get in? How? How much money you got? Where you goin'? How old? Where were you last? When did you work last? Three years ago, huh?' Christ, there ain't a question but what he don't ask it. An' he knows danged well we ain't tellin' him everything. We can't. We gotta eat. We can't tell him about every damn chicken we run over an' et."

Blackie nodded. "An' then the man tells you you're a liar. An' he smiles. An' afterwards he gives you a slip a paper with some markin's on it, an' you walk away with your tail between your legs. An' you wish you had a woman, 'cause then you kin fergit and be a big shot fer a minute."

Maury kept his silence. He would first hear them speak before he spoke up. He squinted as he studied them.

Slim leaned forward and stirred the fire with a long stick. "Funny about wimmen. I had a woman once. Was married down in . . . well, I was married, and had a kid. Nuts about 'em. I was as happy wakin' in the mornin' as I was when I went to sleep at night. We had a farm." Slim narrowed his eyes in memory. "The kid . . . why, the kid was so high. Had white hair, an' burnt gold by the sun. And there was trees full a leaves and the grass was deep and full a bugs, and the sky was either full of rain or sunshine. Well . . . it's all gone now. Disappeared."

Shorty was silent for a while, apparently waiting for Maury.

But Maury waited.

So Shorty said, as he loosened his shoe and rubbed his calloused foot with a tired gesture, "One thing a man must never do. Never go near the goddamn dust bowl. People are friendly there, but they ain't got nothin'." Shorty paused, then went on softly, "Friendly enough, but they ain't got a goddamn thing even for themselves, let alone handin' it out to other guys. You get goddamn mad out there and you get sad. Mad because there the

186

man givin' you help needs it more than you do. And sad because the people are like a pore houn' dog about dead who's still willin' to share a petrified bone he's found."

Maury could hold himself no longer. He hunched forward and squinted into the fire. He waved an arm, and said, "You don't need to tell me about the dust bowl. I know all about the dust bowl. I know it in Oklahoma and I know it in South Dakota. Down in Dakota you come on from the Sioux River there. You come on. First, the land is pretty good, some mighty good, and then it's only a little burnt an' the farmers an' the cattle got a little grub yit. But you come on some more, an' after a while it starts. Why! mile after mile! I know it. I saw it. It was a turrible thing to see. All that, and nobody there, where the land was once full a grass an' corn an' wheat an' cows an' horses. Where there was wimmen hangin' clothes on the line, an' farmers spittin' tobacco juice faster'n any grasshopper ever did. An' kids playin' and young bucks sparkin'. I tell you, it grieves a man's heart to see it." He paused. "An' it wouldn't be so bad if it'd always been desert. But it hain't been. It's been God's land once, an' now it's the Devil's."

Blackie asked, "Did you find any good places to eat there?"

"Well, one . . . well, no."

"Where was it?"

"I said 'No'."

Shorty nodded. "Yeah, that country ain't no goddamn good. Why! even the salesmen there look more like muskrats caught in a trap than human bein's in business."

The others sat silently. Slim rolled a cigarette and passed the makings to Shorty. Shorty rolled one and then passed them on to Blackie. When he finished, he handed them back to Slim with a grunt of thanks.

Maury waved his hands. His eyes were open and luminous and fiery with the light of the flames. "What's gonna happen? This can't go on. Somethin's gotta happen. This runnin' like we're doin', that ain't the answer, either." Then, "I'm tellin' you, fellas, it's awful back there. Gray dust, white bones, people bleedin' white blood, people hackin' an' coughin' . . . what's gonna happen?"

"Dust," Slim whispered, "dust." And his voice crept into the night as hesitantly as a light wind.

Shorty said, "Why, it's so dry there, even the wimmen can't give back a man his seed, let alone the land can't."

"No, I suppose not," Maury murmured, remembering Pa Thor's story.

Fires gleamed on both sides of the railroad tracks like red pinpricks. Shadows moved between them. There was an occasional sound of a clanking tin. Voices murmured like willow branches in water.

Then Shorty leaned over from his crouch and touched lightly on Maury's guitar bundle. "Do you play that, bud?"

"Why . . . a little." Then, "But I don't play much fer others."

"Play it," said Shorty.

"Well . . ."

"Play it," said Slim, bending his eyes upon Maury. "Play it."

And Maury, swallowing, knowing he could not retreat from them, unfastened the bundle and took up the instrument. He fumbled with it, humming the strings a little, fussing with the pegs, and then slowly began.

He sang low at first, and then strummed it hard—

> *I've reached the land of desert sweet,*
> *Where nothing grows for man to eat.*
> *You have no wheat, you have no oats,*
> *You have no corn to feed your shoats.*

188

O Dakota land, sweet Dakota land,
As on thy fiery soil I stand,
I look across the plains
And wonder why it never rains,
Till Gabriel blows his trumpet sound
And says the rain's just gone around.
A-round . . .

I've reached the land of hills and stones
Where all is strewn with buffalo bones.
O buffalo bones, bleached buffalo bones,
I hear your moans, I hear your groans.
'Lo bones . . .

The men nodded, humming with him.

Then Maury, lifting his face and closing his eyes, dreamed, and weaved a new tune, singing—

I got to go up and father up the herd,
I got to go up and fork me on a saddle,
The wolves are aprowl and the bobcat's stirred,
It's time to go up and father up the cattle.

There was a long, thin whistle. The westbound freight. The men stiffened. They groaned as they stood up and picked up their bundles. They slumped away silently. They did not look back. Their backs darkened as they hunched away toward the tracks in the black of the night. The train whistled again. There was a little stir of men. The wind sighed in the telegraph wires. There was an eddy of men moving toward the tracks. The train screamed.

Maury was a little stunned by their heartless leave-taking. It was a strange world. Everybody shared his food, but no one cared much if one was unhappy. He had the feeling that he had supped with dogs who, hearing the master's whistle, had gone off, each leaving the others to their fate.

He watched the backs of the men humping away into

189

the dark. He was struck by the notion that not one walked as straight and proud as did old Pa Thor. These homeless wanderers had, as Pa Thor would say, "narrer backs."

Maury sat alone. He waited for the whistle of a freight going east.

XVII

HE HAD STARTED BACK.

The next night he sat waiting his turn in a relief station. A slouchy man behind a railing looked stiffly at a young man uneasy in poorly-fitted, new clothes. Maury watched him closely and listened to the interviewer.

"What's your name?"

"James Atkins, sir."

The man at the desk stared at his clothes. "When did you get in?"

The young man's voice was soft and timid. "Just now, sir."

"How?"

"Caught a ride with a trucker."

"Have you been here before?"

"No."

"Where you goin'?"

"Milwaukee."

"What for?"

The man hesitated. "Well, to work."

The hard man looked at him and then wrote on a paper. "Where'd you work last?"

"South Dakota."

"Where were you the last five years?"

The timid man was silent.

"Where?"

"Sioux Falls."

"All five years?"

"Yes."

"What did you do there?"

"I . . ." The man quavered.

"What?"

"I . . . well, I left the state pen yesterday."

The hard man looked up suddenly. He jerked back. His eyes narrowed. "Jailbird!" he exclaimed involuntarily.

The timid man recoiled.

The hard man asked, "How come?"

The timid man was silent.

"How come? 'Course it ain't none of my business, but how come?"

"Stole some money."

"Oh?"

The timid man suddenly unwound himself. He talked swiftly. "My gal . . . we were with a traveling show, you see, an' she got into trouble, baby comin', an' we couldn't have it 'cause she was in an act. An' so I got her some stuff, an' she started bleedin', an' she needed a doctor quick, an' so I had to get money quick, an' the boss had some, an' we took it an' he sent me up."

"And the girl?"

"Died."

"Oh." There was a deep, awkward silence. Maury leaned forward, cupping his ear in his hand to listen.

"Whatcha gonna do in Milwaukee?"

"I got a fella there who wrote me an' said I could truck for him."

The hard man asked suddenly, "They gave you some money when you went out, didn't they?"

"Yes."

"Where is it?"

The timid, thin young man's eyes filled.

"Where is it?"

"Sent it to my gal's mother."

The hard man swelled. "Well, we can't help you if you give your money away foolishly. You've got to learn

to take care a yourself first. Naw, you got good clothes
. . . I dunno. No."

The thin man stood near the desk as if he hadn't
heard.

"Go. I told you 'No.' "

The thin man looked at him softly, accusingly, and
then went timidly out of the door.

"Next?"

Maury stood up. He had made a move toward the
desk, but now he abruptly turned to the door.

"Next?"

"Naw," said Maury to the stiff-necked man. "Naw, I
kin get along without your help."

He walked out into the evening. Other men were
crowding around the door for a handout. "Where's the
nearest railroad yards?" Maury asked.

One of them, a shagged, wretched creature, who resembled Ol' Gust, pointed. "Down there. Five blocks."

"Any trains goin' east?"

"Where to?"

"South Dakota."

"You goin' there?"

"I asked a question. Any freights goin' to South Dakota?"

"Yeh. Red-ball at midnight. Catch it on the hump east
a town."

"Thanks," said Maury, curtly. He walked stiffly away.
"Christ!" he exclaimed to himself as he walked along,
"Christ, there ain't no humans anymore anywhere."

XVIII

Maury heard the echoes clambering up the side of the hills and meeting in a long whining snap above him. Smoke whirled past the open door of the boxcar he was in and sometimes a whiff of it came through the door and made him cough. Long irregular, tuftless buttes sprawled away from him toward the southwest and lifted toward the horizon. The sun, as it neared sunset, began to lay out blankets of purple in the ravines and arroyos, and caught the corners of the blankets on the thin red buttes.

He braced himself against the side of the open door. He yawned a few times and ran his fingers through his hair, adjusted his cap deep over his eyes and stretched. He felt for his sack of tobacco, thumbed loose a thin paper, and carefully rolled a cigarette in the hot tugging wind, ending his rolling motion with a flourish and a quick lick of his tongue. He lighted it behind tightly cupped hands.

The train groaned suddenly and whipped the car outward as it rounded a long curve. He held his body tight against the outward push. For a moment he felt he was losing his balance. He froze his muscles. After what seemed an interminable wait, the train straightened its body and the smoke-spouting, probing nose leaped through an opening in a small sleepy village almost obscured by a pall of dust, and he regained his balance. The slowly releasing pull of the momentum was a good feeling. Maury tried to catch the name of the town on the depot, but the lurching freight was too swift. A few seconds later, switch tracks crackled beneath him.

He scanned the sky and tried to peer over the long snake of cars for a sign of driving dust. Though they were approaching the Bad Lands, near where the dust rose easily, the air was still clear. Apparently there was no wind up over the land.

He looked across the boxcar and studied a sleeping man, curled on his side, lying against the far wall, his arm beneath his head. Occasionally, in the quieter moments of the train's rush, Maury could hear him snore.

Maury was impatient to be home, to talk to Pa Thor again, to watch him rub his leg and scan the skies for a cloud, to see Ma Thor fumbling lovingly about her work . . . and to see how his Kirsten was making it. He wondered how his coming would strike them, how they would behave when he returned.

The train suddenly pulled the other way, and Maury had to grip the sides of the door to keep from falling inside on the boxcar floor. Then it straightened again.

He pondered on the days to come. There were a lot of things to do on that Thor farm. He would have to see whether the dam still held water, and whether the greens had held out. He wondered whether the little pigs were still alive, and whether the cow had been bred. Maybe they should dig another well. He had read somewhere that farmers were now jetting three-inch bores straight down for three or four thousand feet through conglomerate until they hit sandstone, until the water couldn't help but flow. He wondered if Ol' Gust had the equipment to drill that deep.

Maury looked out. He examined the land. It unrolled before him like a wide roll of paper. It was leveling into long swells now. He recognized Cedar Butte and Big Foot Hill. There was dust in the air too. He saw a few cactuses and an occasional collection of ambling tumbleweeds. They were near Long Hope.

Maury mused on his old days. He was a farm boy. He liked the morning dew on the greens. He liked to stop his work to look at the birds in the leafy trees. He liked to walk among the cattle and pat their backs and stroke their heads. He remembered the day he had tamed a white-faced bull with his bare hands; the bull had tried to gore him when he had gone walking alone in the fresh wet pasture.

Maury clenched his fist. He had done something terribly wrong. He had, for four years, doubted the land. In the years to come, he would work doubly hard to make the earth, and his own heart, forget that he had been unfaithful.

He heard a cough behind him. He turned. The other man had awakened. As Maury listened to the monotonous beat of the wheel trucks cracking on the splicings of the rails beneath, he studied the man.

Slowly and methodically, as if his body were a machine, the man rose in the dark and stumbled toward Maury.

"Howdy," greeted Maury.

The man stood looking out of the door with bleary, uncomprehending eyes. "Where are we?"

"A couple a miles from Long Hope."

The other nodded, and when Maury reached in his pocket to have another smoke before he leaped off the freight train, the man reached for the papers and the tobacco as if he had a right to them. The man rolled his cigarette with jumpy fingers. He swayed to counteract the roll of the freight. Tobacco spilled in the wind. The suction of the train's speed whipped the grains through the open door. The man held a flame behind cupped hands and then looked out of the door. Then he surveyed Maury, looking at his shoes, overalls, shirt and cap. He glanced at the two bundles near the door.

"Lotta dust out there," the man said impersonally.

"Oh, not so much. Some, but not bad."

The other nodded. He glanced at Maury's overalls again and then looked out of the door, puffing his cigarette, swaying against the other side of the door.

Maury asked, "Where you goin'?"

The man's eyes raised suddenly, held Maury's fleetingly, and then dropped. He was silent.

"Where you goin'?" Maury repeated.

The other looked up and asked, a bit sharply, "You're a farmer, ain't you?"

Maury looked surprised. "How'd you know?"

The man puffed. "Saw you lookin' out the door, watchin' the farm country."

"Aw," said Maury, "lots a fellas do that."

"Yeah?" the man smiled sadly. "Well, not like you."

Maury was resentful. "What do you do?" he asked derisively.

"Nothin'."

"I mean, did do?"

"Pharmacist."

"Drugstore?"

"Yeah." The man clamped down on his cigarette and looked out again.

The two men stood watching the running ground. One stood against the right side of the door, tall, a little bewildered. The other stood shamblingly, his belly hanging loosely in his pelvic sling, his knees bent, his neck curved forward, his face expressionless, his eyes staring straight ahead.

"Where you goin' now?" Maury asked.

The man moved a little, as if in response to the question, and then pinched his cigarette between jumpy brown fingers and remained wordless.

Maury fidgeted against the door. He felt low again.

The man asked suddenly, flipping the words off his shriveled lips, "Goin' home, sonny?"

Maury ignored the last word. "Yeah," he said, swiftly happy again as he remembered the family, and Kirsten, "yeh, how'd you know? Why sure, I'm goin' home!"

The man looked up quickly. He was startled. His eyes dug into Maury's face.

Maury got a sharp picture of the man's surprise at his words. Maury looked out of the door. The train was slowing. And then the houses of Long Hope appeared ahead. He looked eagerly beyond the buildings toward the east. "Long Hope, Long Hope, here I come." Maury picked up his guitar case, tucked it under his arm carefully, and got ready to throw out his other bundle.

The other's eyes quirked sideways and looked quizzically at Maury. And then he suddenly said, "Yeah?"

Maury had already started a forward motion to leap out of the train when the man's word caught him, imprisoning him for a moment. He stared at the man, his face working. He hung balancing in the doorway. Then the boxcar lifted slightly and he flipped out. His bundle of clothes cleared above him. Maury turned his body in the air. He landed on his back and tumbled over. His arm protected the guitar. He heard its strings hum and he could feel their vibration against his body. He tumbled through the ditch and landed against a fence post. He held himself together, waiting for more. He held his head deep down on his chest. Then, surprised that the bruising was over, he looked up to see the caboose of the freight rattling past him. Far ahead, the open boxcar began to round the curve into Long Hope. He could see the lonely figure of the man standing negligently in the doorway looking backward at nim.

Maury stood up and brushed his overalls. He looked around for his other bundle and found it behind a boulder. Then he opened the guitar case. The guitar was unharmed. He looked for a path, and then, crawling between the strands of the wire fence, stepped toward the outlying buildings.

In a few moments he was walking east through town. It was near suppertime and few were on the streets. Late storekeepers were closing their stores, rolling up the awnings and sweeping away the debris that had collected before their shops during the day.

He hurried toward the outskirts of the town, studying the winding road that ran down a slight roll in the land. Ahead, at a curve, a filling station nestled and there he decided to thumb for rides until sundown.

He set down his bundles and pulled back his cap, facing the sun, smiling and stiffening his back. Presently, a low-slung car raced toward him. He waved. But the car went on. Impatient, he waited a few more minutes. Another car came. The driver eyed him coldly, staring at his dusty, faded overalls. Then he too drove on, spurting the car. Maury thumbed his nose after the car. Another car came along. The driver had seen him standing, and now, as he approached, carefully accelerated the car into swiftness, staring the other way, as if he had not noticed Maury. Maury thumbed him too.

"Feelin' pretty gay, ain't you?"

Maury whirled.

There stood Ol' Gust, smiling, in the driveway of the filling station.

"Howdy! Ol' Gust!" Maury ran toward him, his hand extended. He was flooded with joy. "Ol' Gust!"

Ol' Gust shook hands with him, and then quirking his eyes, asked, "Goin' back?"

"Yeh."

Ol' Gust rubbed his whiskers. "Well, now that's good. I heared you'd gone. Pa Thor tol' me a couple a weeks ago. Was sorry to hear it. Well, now, you aimin' to catch a ride there?"

Maury nodded.

Ol' Gust smiled shrewdly. "How much would it be worth to y'u if I took you home?"

"Well . . ." Maury laughed good-humoredly. "Well, I dunno."

Ol' Gust prodded him. "How much?"

"Well, since I can't pay the price fer what it's really worth to me, I'm not even goin' to think of it."

Ol' Gust studied his face and then spat lustily to the left. "Now, that's the way to talk! I like to hear that." Ol' Gust's eyes narrowed on a hidden thought.

"They're still there, ain't they?" Maury asked anxiously.

Ol' Gust spat again. "You know, that's the dangest thing I ever seen. Them hangin' on like bulldogs. Never lettin' go. 'Course, this week ain't been so bad fer them, but the dust has been ridin' pretty stiff this summer."

"I know." Then Maury asked, "You said you had a ride fer me?"

"Yeh. That's right. Soon's I get my tin lizzie oiled up. Feller's oilin' it up back there." Ol' Gust looked slyly around at the premises and winking at Maury, slid a small bottle into his hand. "Reckon you need a little snort to pick you up, huh?"

Maury shook his head.

"No? Still on the straight an' narrer? Well!"

The station attendant beckoned. Ol' Gust walked over to the greasing pit. Then he called, "Feller's got her ready."

Soon they were on the road. Maury fretted. He pushed his feet against the floorboards to hurry the car along. He thought the old Ford was as slow as a tame horse.

Ol' Gust held the wheel loosely. He searched in his

shirt pocket for his plug of tobacco, found it, bit off a corner, and, after chewing it smackingly a few times, asked, "Where'd you go, son?"

"Montana."

Ol' Gust nodded. "Great sheep country."

Maury was irritated at the slow-moving Ford. He was not in a mood for talk. But then he remembered that Ol' Gust drilled wells. "Say, you still got your drillin' outfit?"

Ol' Gust squinted at him. "Yeah, I still got it. Why?"

"Oh, I was thinkin' that if Pa Thor needs water, we oughta drill another well. This time we'll jet one down. A three-incher."

Ol' Gust said shortly, "Kin he afford it?"

Maury nodded, squinting. "Sure."

"Well, it won't do much good. Just a waste a time. 'Sides, the damn machine is pretty well wore out. Don't think it'll stand much more drillin' in this goddamn stone country." Ol' Gust watched the road.

They drove along for a few miles. Then Ol' Gust asked. "Lot a dust up there? Up in Montana?"

"Some."

Ol' Gust nodded. "Yeh. Yes, it's pretty bad up there. I know. Dust and sand hangs on the grass an' weeds so thick it wears the sheeps' teeth down."

"Say," Maury said presently, "say, I guess the sand would at that."

Ol' Gust laughed. "Ever hear the story of the rich feller livin' in Sioux Falls who owned a ranch in Montana? Well, he never saw the ranch, never came west a the city there. And he hired a guy to run it fer him. Well, sir, one time the foreman wrote the rich feller, tellin' him that the sheep was dyin' a starvation 'cause the dust and the sand on the grass had wore their teeth out. Well, the rich feller got to worryin' an' finally he asked a dentist friend a his if he could fix up some sets a teeth fer the sheep. The dentist thought he was kiddin', and so he says, sure, send down a couple a head and I'll make a fittin'."

Maury waited. "Yeah, then what?"

Ol' Gust sluiced a brown jet of tobacco into the side-wind. "One mornin' the dentist gets a big package, an' opens it, an' finds three nice sheep heads. Ripe."

Maury settled back in the seat and laughed.

Ol' Gust went on. "Sure. That really happened! Stunk so bad they had to throw 'em out the winder."

They laughed together.

Ol' Gust looked owlishly through the windshield as he drove along. "Heard any good jokes on the road?"

"No. No, not one."

"You must have your ears plugged. No stories?"

"No."

Ol' Gust mumbled to himself.

Then Maury sighted a side-road ahead. It led off to Sweet Grass where Ol' Gust lived. "You kin let me off here."

"I kin take you all the way."

Maury felt embarrassed. "I'd kinda like to walk the rest a the way by myself an' surprise 'em on the yard. You know, nobody around."

Ol' Gust lowered his eyes. He nodded. "Okay."

Then the road corner appeared in the short valley. The car rounded the turn. Maury got out. "Thanks a lot, Ol' Gust. See you soon."

Ol' Gust waved his hand. "That's all right, son." He shifted the gears and the car seemed to stretch itself and then crawl droningly up the slight incline. A stray cactus leaf lay on the road. A rear wheel crushed its juicy flesh and its clean water washed the dust from a few gravel stones.

XIX

MAURY HURRIED TO THE TOP of the rise and looked eastward. The willows lining the creek were completely bare of leaves. The cottonwood was white-gold in the leveling slashes of sunlight. Beyond the creek, Maury could see a thin curling wisp of smoke rising from the house, becoming whiter as it curled against the oncoming dark purple of the night rising in the east.

Then Maury turned. The rim of the earth had cut the sun in half. The upper half palpitated momentarily before it slid out of sight. Then scarlet light streamed up over the rim of the earth.

Maury crawled through the barbed-wire fence and hastened across the field. He looked anxiously for a sign of some movement on the yard, but there was only the thin coils of white smoke twisting above the shack.

A dying wind scuffled up a little dust in his face, and he stopped a few times to wipe his mouth and eyes. The wind soughed over the tops of the hollow steel posts and drifted dust onto the small banks on the lee side.

Then he entered the field where, when he had last seen it, grain had been greening. There was nothing left now. He hurried toward the creek. The water was gone. Huge, gaping cracks straggled over the baked, brittle ground where once there had been enough water to wash his feet. A few white minnow skeletons flaked its black bottom. He glanced toward the curve where he and Kirsten had been together. Then, with a leap, he bounded through the path in the willows and gained the level land nearer the house. He ran a few steps and then, not to appear too impatient, slowed his walk.

Twice he came upon splits in the topsoil wide enough to engulf a cow or a horse. When he leaped across them, the edges crumbled a little.

He neared the yard. The two horses, Becky and Beaut, were munching in the outdoor feeding rack. Maury saw that the hay was pure tumbleweed. There were no tufts of grass to give the animals a fleeting memory of olden days.

The two cows, thin, gaunt, looked at him forlornly. They were on the west side of the barn and their red hair caught the sunset. Except for their craning heads as they watched him enter the barn, they stood motionless.

He looked anxiously for the old sow. But he found only the seven pigs, now thin, starved. They were too weak to rush the pighole all at the same time.

Cautiously, he opened the door on the other side of the barn. It opened onto the houseyard and he wondered if the greens were gone. He looked around. There were a few; just a few in the shade of the toolshed.

Suddenly he jerked up. Along the edge of the shed, a gaping crevasse had opened. It was jagged and ran irregularly toward the barn.

He studied this new crack in the earth. Near the barn, where the old path had been, Pa Thor had laid down a wide board across it. The split was almost two feet wide, and deep enough to lose a telephone pole. It wriggled in from the field to the north and, cutting across the yard, scissored out to the south.

A little sadly, he closed the door behind him. Then, crossing the fissure on the plank, he started for the house.

There was no sound in the twilight. The red sundown was deepening into purple dusk.

He hurried to the door and knocked.

The door opened. Kirsten. She looked at him; her mouth opened a little. "Why . . . why . . . why . . ."

She whispered the words.

"Hello," Maury greeted. He looked at her. His eyes searched hers, dropped to her body, and returned to her eyes again. Then he knew. In the momentary exchange of glances, she answered his unasked question. He rubbed his nose and looked down to one side.

Kirsten swept back her hair. Then she said calmly, "Well, just in time for coffee."

Maury held himself stiffly. He swallowed quickly. Then he stepped inside.

Ma Thor, sitting at the table, darning, looked up, and then looked toward Pa Thor.

Pa Thor, sitting by the window, smoking his corncob pipe, turned and stared at him. His eyes suddenly filled with astonishment. At a loss for words, he rubbed his leg.

Maury looked at each of them, and then set his bundles near the door. He noticed that they hadn't stored his cot.

It was near bedtime when he and Kirsten stepped outdoors for a moment. Her calm manner all evening had made him apprehensive. He waited for her to speak.

She told him of the summer they had had. There had been no rain. The grain and the corn leaves had curled into themselves, protectively at first, becoming limp and tough and pale green. But the continued beating of the hot sun had burnt the roots and dried the earth into hard layers of near-stone, just as he had predicted. Slowly, thin strips of dead yellow had crept along the edges of the leaves. The tips had become brown, then black. Only the central stem had remained green for a time. The morning dews had kept these alive.

It was only in the early morning that the Thors had sometimes witnessed a trace of the prairie's old glory.

For a brief moment, before the sun came up, the earth had been cool and most of the dust had settled. The half-dark had hid the terrible ugliness of the scalped earth.

But by noon, the sun had come up over the earth's inflamed breast again and had curdled it with heat. The breath of dew had vanished.

Then the Tropical Continental Wind from the south had come, steadily, remorselessly, steadily increasing its power during June and July, insistently wearing at the dried leaves, drying the stems, too, and tearing the leaves loose from them and scattering them into fine bits, until the dark stems stood up like strands of rusted wire.

Once more all the old fissures in the earth had yawned, and new cracks wrinkled away in every direction from them. Some nights the Thors had heard the land booming as it split open, as if ice on a sea were going out. Near the village of Sweet Grass a fissure had opened so wide and so deep that the townsfolk had named it The Bottomless Pit.

By the end of the summer, Ma Thor had run out of things to patch. Pa Thor had put on his last overall and shirt, and she could patch these only when he went to bed. She had spent most of her time dusting the house until she had become almost crazed with the work.

During these days Pa Thor had sat in his rocker by the window most of the time. Sometimes his chair had creaked louder than the creaking of the house bowing in the wind. Most times he sat like a statue, staring to the west. Sometimes he forgot to light the pipe that jutted from the tight lips of his unshaven face.

Immediately after Maury had left, the cattle well had gone dry. The Thors had had to ration the water from the house pump among the animals and the greens and themselves.

The chickens had been eaten. All of them. The bindlestiffs wouldn't be able to steal them any more. There was no more crowing in the mornings.

And the sow had been sold. Ma Thor had bought some food with the money. The last of the staples were in the pantry now.

For a while the pigs got the last milk Kirsten could milk from the two cows. The pigs had been their hope. With a shortage of meat everywhere because of the drouth, the pigs would bring a fancy price on the market, enough to buy a good store of flour and lard and salt and yeast. But now, well, Maury could see. The pigs were very thin.

And Kirsten? Each day Kirsten had become thinner. Though she walked in the sun, she had paled a little. Each day she had watched the west where the road disappeared from sight beyond the bare-armed willows and the gaunt cottonwood. Often she had sat by the side of the window-box in which the geranium stalks had died long ago. Each day she had leaned in it on her elbow. The stealthy dust along the horizon had seemed alive to her, as if it were full of Maurys, each Maury rising out of the earth and stamping his long-armed way toward her.

Maury listened to her grimly, his own mind supplying things she did not say directly. He stood looking at her, then at the dark sky, at the winking stars. For a time they were both silent.

She moved beside him. Her hand was upon his arm. "You gonna stay now?"

Maury mumbled a little.

She stared down at her feet a moment and then said, "Well, anyway, you know the rest. You got a son comin'."

"Yeah, I know." He was silent. "An' in this desert!"

Then he added, "Well! couple a more kids and we'll put that consolidated school back to work again."

Before Maury went to sleep he lay a long while, thinking, brooding.

He listened to the wind as it tugged at the house. He fancied that the gale was rising. Sometimes the shack pitched like a boat, sometimes the floor dipped like a raft.

After a long while, near midnight, he fell asleep.

XX

It is a spectacle to see the great earth dying.

Slowly the drouth wrinkles the skin of the old creature. The veins, the hidden rivers and once-welling springs, dry up. The subsoil becomes brittle, and crumbles, and caves in. The topsoil crumbles, too, and collapses. And crevasses open the body.

Meanwhile, the wind pounds the black skin into fine bits of gray. It bears the rich soil away, hurling and scattering it afar. Soon the deep sands and clays lie exposed.

The stones and the boulders that the earth has held warmly for millions of years become traitors. They split and curve the wind into sharp, whirling, tearing eddies. The hot wind varies; sometimes it is fierce, sometimes it is gentle, sometimes it is sudden. The sand cuts the earth. The gullies widen. Sand dunes rise and billow. Drifts move slowly in the lee of the boulders and the posts and the stones, back and forth, beside and above the buildings and the machines and the graves of men.

And then a desert drifts where once a home had been tucked away in a valley. The weeds and the seeds of the weeds fail. Brittle green and red-gray tumbleweeds roll and toss over the dunes, over the wounded subsoil. The gray dust and the sand mix with the red-brown soils of the buttes and the yellow clays of the gullies. The heated alkali is pulverized, and the earth begins to smell.

The lingering taste of the sour alkaline almost embitters the people, though resentment at the land they have loved rarely bursts into flames. They look with wry wonder at the gray land under their feet and the land flying high in the sky above them.

Even before the sun was up, a full hour, the Big Wind came. From Mexico and across Arizona the hot dry wind came northward with its licking tongue. Like a prairie fire, it scorched all growing things. It boiled up the dust on the parched land.

Dust charged the mountains, fell upon the gutted prairies, droned across Colorado and Nebraska, tumbling, twisting, cutting, spilling, over the knolls and the buttes, stirring the silt of the Dakotas.

The broad feet of the wind lumbered through the valleys, leaping the rivers: the Platte, the White, the Bad, the Cheyenne, the Little and the Big Sioux, the Missouri, stumbling over the Dakotas.

The dry hot wind lashed at the breasts and shoulders of the land. Soon huge dust eddies ran swiftly along the road. Whirlwinds scurried on the paths of the fields and scruffed the bark of the roadside willows. The hot wind moaned in the cracks of the house, sometimes shrilly, sometimes hoarsely, moaning and crying against the house. Towers of dust rose blackly in the night.

The dry wind ran swiftly northward. It screamed in the cottonwoods along the rivers. The thin rivers shrank. They lay pale in the clay. Gray velvet covered them gently behind the windbreaks. They lay ill. The earth lay gray. The dry wind filled its lungs with dust.

Maury was awakened by a dull pain in his right eye. He did not awaken suddenly. The pain gradually wrestled sleep to the ground. He blinked. As he did so, he could feel the dust cascade off his nose into the lashes on either side. The pain in the eye sharpened when he cautiously moved his eyeballs. He guessed that a fine piece of glass-like sand had drifted in and had lain there, cutting into his eye as it rolled a little in his dream. Suddenly, whipping his head to one side and then rolling over on his side, he shook the dust from his face. Then he swung his legs over the edge of the bed.

He was startled by the amount of dust in the house. There was more than an inch of it on the floor. In his mouth the tiny particles gritted between his teeth.

He shook his head and then rubbed his eye. The pain was very sharp now. He thought of reaching for his red handkerchief, but realized that it, too, would be full of dust and sand that would fill his eyes even more.

He coughed, and then discovered that the dust had drifted into his mouth and filmed his throat. He coughed hard. It was curious the way he was discovering things, one by one, in his sleepy state. Even the mind was slow to waken these days.

Then he heard the roaring outside and knew that it had come. The Big Wind. The Big Dust. Perhaps a Black Blizzard again.

The shack shook. His bed moved. His mind became alert. Little drafts came through the window-casing and blew dust on his back.

A hoarse cough shook him. He wondered what was happening to the fine pink tissues of his lungs. He recalled vividly the time he and Pa Grant, in Oklahoma, in butchering a pig, had cut up the lungs to see what they were like. They had been pink in spots, purple in others; and wonderfully soft, like a woman's breasts. Again a cough rumbled within him.

He cautiously rolled his eye once more. He squinted. The pain was very sharp and his whole sentient being was concentrated on it. He mused on the idea of wetting a fingertip with saliva and letting a drop of moisture run into his eye. It might wash that bit of sand away. He coughed, trying to raise some moisture. But his mouth was too harshly dry. Even his sucking tongue could not gather up spittle.

There was a sharp, lightning-shaped flash of yellow where the sand lay cutting away. He had a quick vision of it. It would be like a weasel in the night, cutting away on the neck of a chicken and sucking it dry of blood.

He rolled his eyes at the thought of the snake-agile weasel and, by a lucky roll, drew the sand out of its hole. Then, miraculously, the pain was gone. He rolled his eyes experimentally, feeling wonderfully relieved and yet not sure that he had dislodged the sandgrain. But the sharpness was gone. He winked his eyes. His right eye was watering now.

Then he concentrated on the idea of the Big Dust. He coughed, and knew that it was time to wake the rest of the family. If the storm kept up much longer, they would choke to death in their sleep. He had been lucky to have had a bit of sand come into his eye. Otherwise, his throat and nose might have drifted shut. He grinned to himself about the fancy.

He drew on his clothes and stood up and shuffled through the dust on the floor. It lay unevenly. In some places the floor was bare, in others it was ridged with miniature mounds and drifts three or four inches deep. He shuffled through them across to the back-room door. He opened it quietly and looked in. He could see nothing. It was black. He hesitated. Ma Thor had been the one to be up the night of the other dust storm. What had happened that she wasn't up now, like a brood hen watching her family? Perhaps too worn out to care any more.

Well, it was time now for the young to carry on. The young. Kirsten was the young mother now. He would call her. He hesitated again. A wonder grew in him about the child nestling in her belly. How large was it now? What was its shape, size? Did it feel by now?

Then he called her. She appeared in a few moments.

He closed the door behind her and drew her toward the kitchen table. Then he thought of the lamp and he fumbled in his overall pocket for a match. With the utmost caution, in a wind that poured through the house like water through a large-holed sieve, he managed to light the lamp and get the glass chimney over the flame. He turned up the wick and the room became alive with thousands of glinting particles of sand flicking up like fireflies.

The winking light caught upward at her features. She was pale, a little frightened. Her eyes were wide with questioning. "What is it . . . a storm?"

"Yes. Kirsten, you got to wake up the folks and get Pa an' Ma to carry some water in here. Carry in a lot an' cover it up. And then cut rags—"

"I know. We did that before."

"Good. Then I won't need to explain it."

"Where you goin'?"

"Out to the barn. Save the animals. Somebody's got to watch 'em, an' muffle 'em. Somehow, we gotta hang on."

The west window rattled. Then the south and the north windows banged. There was a feeling of suction in the room, and the lamplight sank and fluttered.

"You'll be careful?" she asked.

"Sure." He squinted at her and was almost tempted to kiss her.

She looked at him with misgivings. "Tollef, he . . ."

"Now, my cottontail, now. Don't worry. I know the dust pretty well." Then, "Hurry! Wake up Pa and Ma, an' start shaggin' in a couple a pails a water. Hurry, or it'll be too late." He patted her back. "Get your duds on, an' hurry."

"Ain't you gonna put on a coat?"

"No. Why? The wind is hot. So long, bunny."

He turned quickly away from her, caught up the old

213

lantern by the door, opened the door with a quick, powerful jerk, and hurled himself into the wind. As he pulled
the door after him he saw that the wind rushing in
through the opened door had blown out the light inside.

Bending into the wind, he waited until he saw a small
orange glow at the window again. Then, sure that Kirsten had managed to light the lamp, he turned to fight
his way across the yard.

Two wires led from the side of the house to the barn,
and he went in search of them.

He found the wires. He followed them, bucking ahead,
closing his eyes to mere slits, peering down at the earth.
He could not face the wind directly.

He had the feeling that he was walking along the floor
of an ocean full of black ink. The wild prairie was an
inky ocean roiled by a tempest. Here along the bottom,
where he was shuffling along, it was totally dark. Looking down, or straight on, he could see nothing. The rushing, inky dust moved too swiftly and too thickly to allow an object to radiate the faint luminescence that, for
the sharp-eyed, all objects have in the dark. Looking up,
the black was not quite so black. There was a faint less-
ening in its intensity, the faintness that a man would see
if he looked up from the bottom of an ocean.

Long black veils coiled and slithered above him.

He moved along cautiously.

Then he heard a heavy thump. Another. It came closer. Suddenly, and he hadn't thought the night could be
any blacker, he saw it darken in front of him, concen-
trate fearfully before him. The great thumping, like a
stalking sky-giant, was right upon him, and then roared
past him, and disappeared with the wind into the night.
As it passed, with a violent wrench, the object ripped
the barbed-wire out of his hand. Fright stiffened him in

his tracks. He opened his eyes a little. The dust and cutting sands stung his tender eyeballs.

Then he knew what it was, and he bent over and smothered a nervous laugh. It had been the privy. The wind had uprooted the privy.

The right hand that had held the barbed wire was wet. He rubbed his fingers together. He raised them to his nose. He smelled. Blood. The damned privy had ripped up his hand. He'd have to doctor that up with some of the cattle medicine in the barn before he could begin to carry the water.

And now there were neither stars nor wires to follow. The entire earth had been deluged with a madly rushing flood of black ink.

He could only guess the direction and hoped he would find the barn. Kirsten had been right. A man could get lost in this dust blizzard. It was worse than any night snowstorm he could remember.

He bent over into the wind. He struggled. He fought for what he thought must have been a full hour.

He began to worry that he had missed the barn and the crevasse near it. He stopped, breathing behind his hand. The lantern clanged against his leg. He tried to find a landmark. He kicked at the ground and thought he felt something under his feet. He sank to his knees and, with his dripping right hand, felt around. He was in the middle of the patch of greens. He was going in the right direction then.

He fumbled the sods a little. The wind was tearing them up, rolling them up like carpets.

Something brushed against him. He kicked at it. It was a wildly rolling tumbleweed.

The wind was hot, and sharp with elements. He felt them cutting him.

He got up out of his crouch and staggered ahead, alert

for the crevasse. Somewhere nearby Pa Thor had put a plank across it. He felt ahead with a wary toe. When he could not find it, he wondered whether he had strayed off into the fields to the left or right, where other hungry crevasses awaited him.

But, presently, his toe went off into space. He trembled. The plank should be somewhere near.

He searched for a long time. He was sure he had gone astray in the field. This fissure might be the one he had seen near the dam. Certainly enough time had gone by for him to have wandered that far.

He went a little way farther. Once, a huge chunk broke off the edge. He felt the earth he crouched on sink beneath his weight. He drew in a breath. His heart pounded wildly in his chest. His eyes rolled a little. He leaped back from the sagging terrain. He landed safely on firm ground. Then the broken chunk crashed below, and rumbled in the belly of the earth.

He sat still for a while, steadying his breathing.

When he had quieted his trembling, he went on, searching.

Soon he found the plank. Reassured, he crossed over. Now the barn was but a step away. He searched for the door handle. He opened the door and pulled it closed after him. He stopped to puff a moment and then, hating the dreaded black dark, tried to light the lantern. Two matches failed. But the third caught the wick and he dropped the glass chimney around the flame. It sputtered, and he shook the lantern to splash the kerosene onto the wick roots. The dull orange flame came up bright yellow. Though the air in the barn was smoky with dust, he felt safe. The shadows in the stalls and the stanchions were friends.

He looked about. The two horses, Becky and Beaut, and the two cows were outdoors. But first, his bleeding hand. He went to the medicine cabinet and found some salve, found a rag, and bound up his wounds against the dust.

He went over to the south side of the barn and found the little pigs sleeping. They were huddled in a heap, a tangled mass, piled one on the other. They had tried to bury their noses under each other's bellies. He muttered, "It'll be a helluva job keepin' Kirsten's jiggers from chokin'. They ain't gonna take to them mufflers too good. Won't have brains enough to keep 'em on. Them rootin' fools."

He entered the alley to hang up the lantern so that the light would shine into both the horse stalls and the cowbarn. As he was about to hang up the lantern on a nail, he saw the nail move back and forth, slowly, like a lazy pendulum. The barn was rocking. He watched the pulsing movement a moment, and then muttered to himself, "It's a damned good thing Pa built this strong. At that, the barn's probably stronger than the house."

He found the two horses leaning over the barn door on the north side. Since the wind was coming up from the south, he had little trouble opening it and letting the horses in. He patted them as they walked by. They were good horses. They would be right on the job next spring.

Then he closed the door, both the lower and the top halves, latched it tightly, and went over to open the cow door, also on the north side. He had some trouble finding the cows. A few times the doors blew shut before he found them and so he had to go back to hook the doors against the barn again. But, finally, by placing the yard between himself and the open, light-filled doorway, he saw the silhouettes of the cows. They were huddled against each other on the other side of the feedracks, just as he had guessed. They stood dumbly, heads down, backs to the wind. Unlike the horses, they were too stupid to know what was good for them, or to understand what he might want. He had to beat them with a piece of wood that he ripped out of the racks. Reluctantly, they went up before his clubbing.

Stalled and stanchioned, both the horses and the cows seemed numbed in the yellow glow of the flickering lantern light. He looked at them only a moment and then began to fashion a plan to get the water from the house well.

He hunted behind the horse stalls for a piece of rope. When he couldn't find a length, he unhitched the reins from the harness. He tied the leather lines end to end into a long single string. He rolled it up carefully.

He found the old stone crock where Pa Thor stored the salt for the salt-lick. The salt was caked with dust. He tipped the salt into one of the mangers in the second empty stall and then set up the five-gallon crock near the door.

He unhooked the two old watering pails from their pegs on the wall behind the calf-pen and then, fastening one end of the leather line to a post in the barn, opened the door and started to cross the yard, paying out the line as he went along. He fought his way to the plank, over it, and beyond. With some satisfaction he saw that the plank lay directly in a line with the pump and the door.

He fancied once that he heard the house door slam, that he saw a form like Pa Thor's at the pump.

But when he arrived at the house well, half-way across the yard, he found no evidence that Pa Thor had been there. Peering, he tried to see the house in the dark. But the dust was too thick. The faint lamplight in the shack could not penetrate it.

He tied the end of the string to the pump.

The hurricane drove onto him, sometimes pushing

him off the platform as he worked. He drew up one of the pails over the snout of the pump. He pumped rapidly. The wind blew the pail up on its side. He shoved it down and pumped again. He filled both pails.

Then he fitted the guide-line over his left shoulder and, as he moved along underneath it, let the knifing wind blow it against his neck. He followed the whipping and snapping line along. He found the plank, crossed it. The gale whipped at the water and drenched his legs. He found the barn.

He filled the crock finally. He decided he could not leave the guide-line out in the dark to be whipped to shreds by the wind. He opened the door again, crossed the fissure on the plank, followed the line out to the pump, unfastened the knot, and then, returning to the barn, rolled up the line. Then he locked the barn again.

It was odd, he thought then, that it had not lighted outdoors somewhat. The dawn should have come long ago.

He searched the little feedbin to one side of the horse stalls for the strips of sack Pa Thor used to mask the animals. When he could not find them, he took up a couple of whole burlap sacks. They had the musty smell of aged grain. He ripped them into pieces two feet square. Then he soaked them in the water and with them bound the noses of the horses. He had begun to cough and wondered why the horses and cows hadn't coughed. He had heard the pigs whistle a few times.

Both the cows and horses were quiet as he fitted them with the soaked masks. The horses seemed to know what he was about, and the cows were too stupid to protest.

But the little pigs were a problem.

He ripped up smaller squares for them and then, soaking each of seven in the water, went over and tried to mask them too. But the pigs wriggled and rubbed the masks from their snouts. They were rooters, they were, and wanted to keep their working instruments free and ready for action.

He studied them a while and then thought of a plan. He found another sack, this time a large one. He ripped open one side of it to make of it a large blanket, almost four by four, and then, soaking it, covered the entire heap of pigs.

Then he fashioned a mask for himself and, wetting it, sat back on a milkstool to wait out the storm.

He rested. He watched the timbers move around him. He heard the wind drive on the barn. He quelled an impulse to smoke. Sparks would be dangerous now.

The gale held on steadily, solidly, unvaryingly.

A weak light began to creep in at the windows.

It was when the gale had let up a trifle that he decided to see how Kirsten and the family were getting along in the shack. He soaked his mask again and tied it tightly to his face. He blew out the lantern. Instantly the creaking barn became a cellar of sinister blackness.

To avoid the wind, he went out through the horse-barn door. When he came to the corner of the barn, where the wind lay waiting for him, a force grabbed him and almost rolled him over. He leaned into it and started slowly for the house. By bending over in the faint light, he could vaguely see the floor of the prairie ocean. It unsettled him that the day so far advanced could still be dark.

He found the crevasse, found the plank crossing it, and then headed for the house, holding his wet mask firmly to his face.

He had trouble opening the house door. It seemed frozen on its hinges. In a moment he heard Pa Thor trying to help him on the inside. Together they wrestled with the door. Then he entered, choking and coughing. He ripped off the thick web of dirt that had been a wetted mask but a few minutes before.

He found the family dressed. Ma Thor had made coffee, and now brought out some dried bread and cut a few slices for him on the breadboard. Maury ate hungrily, rinsed his mouth with coffee, and then, once more wetting his mask, turned to talk to the family. He rolled a cigarette and smoked it cupped in his hand to keep the sparks from flying.

He had an impulse to laugh. Kirsten, Ma Thor, and Pa Thor, with their anxious eyes peering over the edges of their wet masks, looked like bandits. He waved his bandaged hand and shouted, "I see you got the water."

Pa Thor nodded, and absent-mindedly, tried to put his pipe into his cloth-covered mouth.

Maury grinned.

Pa Thor yelled, "How's the animals?"

"Good. I left them fine."

Kirsten pointed to his bound hand.

Maury shrugged in answer. "It's nothing. Just cut it a little."

They sat looking at each other. It was hard to talk.

Then the jerking winds came up over the land. When they hit the shack he was sure that the bending structure would go, that it would join the privy.

He watched the shack wrestle blindly with its implacable enemy. It staggered and shook and rocked. The timbers creaked loudly.

The Big Wind paused, waited a moment, then came on with a blast that shook the shack even more violently.

Well, he thought grimly, well, let the damned wind blow. If it blows the house down, we'll build another.

He thought about the family of animals in the barn. The horses and cows and pigs had a better refuge than he and the Thors did. The barn had been built of tough cottonwood, the shack of willow.

The windows rang.

He had the distinct feeling that it wasn't a wind they were wrestling with, but a malevolent being, and one of such unmatchable size that, if it wanted to, it could kill them all.

Just the same, Maury thought grimly, the Big Fellow would know he'd been in a fight before he got through with the Thors.

The small shack rocked.

The Big Wind came on, tearing, roaring, shouting.

Maury sat waiting.

The earth thundered about them. He had a feeling that Judgment Day was at hand.

Maury quaked a little.

Then, with the sound of a flashing shotgun, a pane in the window over his cot popped out and the glass splintered through the shack. Pieces of it hit his face.

He jumped up, thoroughly frightened. He quaked. The others stiffened in their chairs. Just before the lamp went out, he saw thick veils of dust driving into the house.

He saw too, just before the flame vanished, the small square breadboard lying on the table where Ma Thor had placed it to cut the hardened bread. He guessed it might cover the opening in the window. He leaped to the stove. Behind it were a pail of nails and a hammer. He grabbed them up and, crawling in the dark, found the breadboard. Vaguely, he was aware that the others were also stirring around in the room.

He held the square of wood over the hole and felt that it fit very well. He held it up as he fumbled for a nail with his bound right hand. He put a few nails between his lips. With his left hand holding the board hard against the opening through which the enemy tried to pour its poisonous dust, he pushed a nail into the wood. He took up the hammer. With a quick, sure swing, he hit blindly in the dark at the nail. He hit at it again and again. He hit until he had driven it deep into the wood.

Now, he thought, now! Let the Big Fellow try again.

The Big Fellow did. With a loud scream, the nails in the door hinges were torn out. The door staggered across the room as if a powerful fist had sent it reeling. It crashed against the table.

Maury shouted. "Hey, Pa. Help me. Grab up the door and help me put it back in place."

He felt Pa Thor fumbling near him. Then Kirsten and Ma Thor, too. Together they carried the door to the threshold where the Big Fellow came thundering through.

"C'mon. Let's keep that big black bastard out!" Maury shouted. "That big black devil ain't gonna do us in. That son-of-a-bitch!" They pushed and slammed the door into place.

"Now hold it hard!"

They held hard. And, leaping, he grabbed the nails and hammer and began to swing beside them.

And then, abruptly, the Big Fellow retreated. The wind stilled. The air rustled with silence. For a second he could hear the waters of an ocean stilling.

Wondering, startled, Maury let the hammer fall to the floor. He looked from Kirsten to Pa Thor to Ma Thor. He pulled the loose door from their fumbling hands and went outside on the stoop to look. He took off his mask.

It was a strange world he saw.

The buildings were just beginning to gather themselves up and shake themselves and resettle their feathers.

Tumbleweeds slowed down.

And there, and everywhere, were new dustdrifts, new dunes, rising, falling, billowing. There had been an enormous shifting of earth.

He looked up. Dust drifted slowly down, circling, wafting toward the earth.

He listened. He heard the heart of the earth beating beneath him.

He looked toward the barn. He could see it but vaguely. Beaut must have broken loose, for now she stood leaning over the lower half of the horsebarn door, looking at him.

Then Kirsten and Pa Thor and Ma Thor came out on the steps too. They came wondering, casting their eyes skyward. They, too, took off their masks.

Maury called out, "Hey!" and was startled to hear an echo "Hey." off the low buildings.

"Hey!" Pa Thor called. "Hey."

It was a child's game.

Maury stepped off the stoop and went a little way into the yard. He waved an arm. "Well, is this all? It sure seems funny, don't it?"

"It sure does," the old man said, looking up at the sky. "I dunno."

"I've been thinkin' that maybe we're in the middle of a cyclone," Maury observed after a while.

"I dunno. Can't tell."

Maury looked around over the flat, billowing prairie. Though the dust was still thick, he could already see some way to every side.

Pa Thor rubbed his leg, and mused, "Say, I wonder, it ain't workin' up to a rain again, is it?"

Maury smiled a little, and shook his head. "No, I don't think so." Then, "Huh! You an' your rains, Pa." He chuckled. "You an' your rains. You never forgot 'em, did y'u?"

"Why!" and now the old man exploded a little and he came down the steps and stood beside Maury. "Why, 'course I ain't!"

"After all this dust, you still remember the rains?"

Pa Thor peered out toward where the horizon became vague. "Why, I kin remember the rains plain as day. Can't you?"

Maury was silent. He glanced at Kirsten, then back to Pa Thor.

Then he walked toward the barn.

*   *   *

In the hidden country of a pilgrim's heart, rains are falling. The sun shines there, and men go into the fields and work, and believe in the work of their hands. And sow grain, and broadcast the seed of grass for their cattle and horses. And plant corn and melon-seed in the gray-black loam.

And the land trembles with multitudes of germinant sprouts growing and leaping in the sun.

And more rains come to interrupt the beating of the sun upon the earth.

The shoots swell and grow and become tall stalks, the grain and the corn and the hay, laden with the burden of milk-heavy fruit. Fat ears grow on the grain, and the stalks bow with the weight of their ripeness, and become golden. And full ears grow on the corn, and the stalks bow with the weight of fat kernels, and they become golden. And legumes flower and fall, and fill the land with the fragrance of new-mown hay.

When harvest-time comes the women and children sing with joy, the children romping around the stacks of hay

225

and grain and shocks of corn, the women gossiping in their kitchens.

And the men sit back and look upon their handiwork, and smoke their pipes, and casually stretch their muscled arms, and yawn. And sometimes smite their thighs in laughter.

Then, when the great Canadian wind comes whooping down from the north, the people congregate in the barns, the one the other, and dance and play and husk the shocks of corn.

Outside, the wind drives the rolling tumbleweeds along, and blows fiercely down the necks of the farms.

And it is safe for the young lads to squire the girls, and to mate, and have children.